Best True
GHOST STORIES
of the 20th Century

DAVID C. KNIGHT

illustrated by Neil Waldman

Simon and Schuster Books for Young Readers
Published by Simon & Schuster Inc., New York

Published by Simon and Schuster Books for Young Readers
A Division of Simon & Schuster Inc.
Simon & Schuster Building
Rockefeller Center
1230 Avenue of the Americas
New York, NY 10020

Designed by Constance Ftera

10 9 8 7 6

10 9 8 7 6 5 4 pbk

Simon and Schuster Books for Young Readers
is a trademark of Simon & Schuster, Inc.
Manufactured in the United States of America

Library of Congress Cataloging-in-Publication Data
Knight, David C.
Best true ghost stories of the 20th century.
Summary: Stories of unexplained events that baffled
psychic researchers, including the Tulip Staircase ghost,
the ghosts of Versailles, the phantom of Howley Hall links,
and others.
1. Ghosts—Juvenile literature. [1. Ghosts.
2. Psychical research] I. Waldman, Neil, ill. II. Title.
BF1461.K585 1984 133.1 83-23075
ISBN 0-671-66556-1   ISBN 0-671-66557-X pbk

CONTENTS

FOREWORD

IN SELECTING AND RETELLING THE TRUE GHOST TALES IN this volume, I have attempted to include a broad spectrum of representative cases from 1900 through 1980. But there has been an overlapping with the nineteenth century, for some cases extending over many years had their origins somewhere in the 1800s and carried on into the present century. I have incorporated a number of these since, in the eyes of many interested in the occult, the last two decades of the nineteenth century were a kind of heyday of lively, provocative real-ghost happenings. Certainly the classic Borley Rectory case ranks high among these.

Readers should also understand that the pieces included here, as events involving actual people, do not read like fiction. Although there are usually principal characters, there are no contrived plots, resolved conflicts, or satisfying endings. Indeed, many of the endings are baffling and inexplicable. The tales are offered as true cases in psychical research, or parapsychology. This science, a division of psychology, deals with behavioral or personal effects that do not fall within the scope of known physical principles. Parapsychologists have a term for these stories: *spontaneous cases.* They are events that simply happened to people—unprompted and unbidden.

The spontaneous cases retold in these pages originated from a number of sources, including the *Journal* of the American Society for Psychical Research, the publications of the British Society, personal files, and other volumes in the wide literature of psychical research. Where possible, original accounts by eyewitnesses were drawn upon; where these were not available, secondary accounts by reliable authors were employed. No attempt has been made to alter basic events in the cases for the sake of a "better story." Where quoted dialogue appears, it was actually spoken, strongly suggested in primary accounts, or would naturally have taken place in the circumstances.

Beyond their mere entertainment value, it is my hope that these case stories will serve a greater purpose: to make readers aware that there are forces operating in dimensions beyond the knowledge of our five senses, and these can sometimes interact with our physical world in strange ways.

Readers should also know something about the kinds of ghosts they will be meeting in these pages. So-called "ghosts" fall into two general categories: poltergeists and apparitions. The former are by far the most common, and many hundreds of cases of them have been reported. *Poltergeist* is a German word meaning "noisy ghost." The true poltergeist is never seen; it is heard and sometimes felt, but only its effects can be observed. Poltergeists specialize in making crashing sounds, knocking on walls, tossing crockery about, rapping and thumping, and performing similar acts. In a strictly scientific sense, there is no such thing as a poltergeist *per se*—not as an actual being or entity, although they are often written about as such. There are only poltergeist *disturbances* or *activities*—odd events caused by some as-yet-unexplained power or force, possibly psychological in nature. Many poltergeist cases have been minutely investigated by trained researchers, who found that they could not be attributed to fraud, trickery, or natural causes.

Often poltergeist activity announces its coming with certain "signal noises," such as rapping sequences, windlike sounds, faint footfalls, or the rattling of door knobs and latches. It can also produce sounds that resemble those of humans, such as moaning, sighing, sobbing, screaming, and dragging footsteps. Poltergeist events seem to run their course for a certain period of time, then they apparently lose their psychic energy and cease. In most cases, they endure for several weeks, but sometimes they have been known to last a year or more. Occasionally there are visual effects, such as ghostly lights and fluorescences. They can yank bedclothes and blankets off; lock and unlock doors; make organs and pianos play; suffuse rooms with perfumes; steal and return keys and coins; produce liquids such as milk or beer; and do many other things.

Disturbances caused by poltergeists can occur by day or by night, indoors or out. Objects involved in poltergeist activity can move about in abnormal ways; for instance, a dish might sail through a room, stop suddenly in midair, and zip off at a right angle—a seeming impossibility. Sometimes these flying objects have been known to hurt people, but they seldom do. Even when an object has struck a person, he or she has often felt no pain. No one knows why. In addition, there have been cases in which witnesses have experienced ghostly forces touching them, lifting them, or even slapping, pinching, pushing, or restraining them. In the parlance of psychical research, these are known as *tactile cases*.

Psychic investigators have found that poltergeist activity tends to center around adolescent boys or girls who are approaching, undergoing, or have recently undergone puberty. Of course this is not always true—the disturbances can center about anyone at all—but it appears to be the general rule. Researchers refer to them as "focus persons"; sometimes the activity follows these young people from one location to another. Often they are going through severe emotional stresses connected with blossoming sexual energies, of which they themselves may not be consciously aware. Investigators are now inclined to believe that in some manner these inner mental stresses may transfer themselves outside the body in the form of energy powerful enough to cause poltergeist events.

For many years researchers have been deeply interested in poltergeist activity and what its ultimate meaning might be. In a number of cases, objects have appeared out of nowhere or have been thrown into or out of closed places. This implies the passing of physical matter through other physical matter—an apparently impossible phenomenon. It also involves *teleportation*; an object is said to be teleported if it is moved from one place to another by other than normal physical means. Yet some theories have been adduced to account for these phenomena. One holds that the moving object is somehow first dematerialized, or "dissolved," during teleportation, then rematerialized at the spot where it turns up and is seen by witnesses.

Another theory is based on the fact that much of physical matter is made up of empty space in its atomic structure; if the atoms of one object—say a brick wall—could be lined up exactly between those of another object—say a baseball— the ball could theoretically pass through the wall. But so far, atomic physics has not suggested how this might be done.

Still another theory involves the idea of a "fourth dimension"—a higher order of space that permits movement in
some other, or "fourth," way that is different from the
three-dimensional reality we are familiar with. However,
modern science has not had much of a concrete nature to say
about such a dimension.

A number of parapsychologists now think that the phenomenon called *psychokinesis*—a term meaning the ability of
mind-directed energy to move objects without any inter-
mediate physical means—is associated with poltergeist activity. Psychokinesis, also popularly known as "mind over matter," is called PK for short. More often than not in poltergeist
cases, the "focus person" is completely unaware that his own
PK is causing the activity. In any event, although PK has
been proven to exist under controlled conditions in parapsy-
chological laboratories, scientists still don't know what it
really is or what makes it happen.

Investigating poltergeist cases is difficult, because the disturbances often don't last very long. Unless a researcher is
on the spot when the events begin, or shortly afterward, his
opportunity is gone. And sometimes the activity ceases completely in the presence of strangers or when the focus person
or persons leave the scene. Moreover, the disturbances usually end as abruptly and unexpectedly as they started.

Concerning the category of ghosts known as apparitions—spirits, phantoms, and the like that can actually be
seen—even less is known. They are far less common than
poltergeist cases, although some cases comprise both apparitional and poltergeistic elements. When seen by observers,
apparitions are usually wispy and transparent; often they
are seen to glide instead of walk. They are witnessed only
briefly and then either vanish or dissolve slowly from view.
But photographs have been taken of apparitions, suggesting

that at least some measure of physical matter—however thin its consistency—was present to register on the film's chemical emulsion. In rare instances, apparitions have been heard to speak and have touched people.

In most cases, apparitions are of people known to be no longer living—a person or persons either long dead or only recently dead. Of the latter, there is a body of cases known as "death-bed visions." In these cases, the spirit or apparition of a dying or recently dead person appears to a loved one or friend, as if bidding a final affectionate farewell. Often the apparition is seen to be smiling, perhaps in anticipation of a better existence to come. In rare instances, the apparition of a living person is seen, when that same person is known to be somewhere else. These are called "double" cases. Also on the rare side are multiple-witness cases, some of which appear in this volume, in which more than one witness sees the ghost. These are valuable to researchers because they confirm that the apparition was really seen by others, whereas a single witness could be acccused of hallucinating.

Psychical research has not provided any real explanation of apparitional ghosts. Often they are simply classified as "visual hallucinations"—a seeming visual perception that has no objective reality. The "death-bed visions" are frequently written off as such. Something—no one knows just what—triggers the observer's sense of sight, and he or she "sees," or believes that he or she sees, the apparition of a dead or dying person. However, this is hardly a satisfactory answer.

Far more rational is the explanation offered by spiritualists and others, particularly followers of Eastern beliefs, that humans—and indeed all living creatures—survive the event known as physical death. They possess a second, or spirit, body—still material but highly attenuated and not usually visible to the human eye—that continues to exist after bodily death. Normally, this second body passes to another dimensional plane where it takes up its new after-death life. But in some cases, newly dead persons—particularly those who have met violent and sudden deaths, perhaps by murder or in war—do not realize what has happened to them. Finding themselves in their new spirit bodies, which resemble the physical ones they have just shed, they are not aware that they have passed through physical death and they continue to linger about the places they knew in life. They are, according to this belief, "earthbound" and on occasion (nobody can explain just how) their spirit bodies can materialize briefly as ghostly apparitions.

Here, then, representing the decades to date of the twentieth century, is a selection of true ghost stories about real people in real situations. Because they occurred at different places and different times, these phenomena share an obvious universality. Furthermore, they are all linked together by the fact that no natural or purely physical explanations can account for them.

As a former Lay Fellow of the American Society for Psychical Research, I wish to thank that dedicated organization for the use of its library facilities and publications. In particular, I would like to thank Mrs. Fanny Knipe, executive secretary of the ASPR, for her patience and invaluable assistance.

David C. Knight
Dobbs Ferry, New York
Spring 1984

THE
TULIP
STAIRCASE
GHOSTS

IN WHAT IS PERHAPS THE MOST REMARKABLE GHOST photograph ever taken, shrouded figures are seen to climb the famous Tulip Staircase in one of the buildings at the National Maritime Museum in Greenwich, England. The photo was taken by a retired clergyman and his wife in 1966.

The museum building in question is the lovely Queen's House. The structure was conceived and built by the noted seventeenth-century architect Inigo Jones for King James I's queen, Anne of Denmark. It was eventually completed and dedicated to Henrietta Maria, queen of King Charles I, after that monarch ascended to the throne.

Throughout the long history of this handsome building, there is no notation in its official records that it is, or ever has been, haunted by ghostly apparitions. Unofficially, however, there is evidence that it is. One official who worked for many years in the Queen's House has said there are stories of a strange figure being seen in the tunnel underneath the pavement just outside the building. A former custodian admitted that he has heard footsteps in various parts of the Queen's House which he cannot logically explain.

In addition, an ex-warder at the Maritime Museum has said that he has often seen mysterious figures that seem to hover around the famed Tulip Staircase. One of the main tourist attractions of the Queen's House, the staircase is so named for the sculpted tulip designs in its iron banister-work.

In the summer of 1966, it was precisely in the vicinity of the Tulip Staircase that an amazing occurrence took place. A retired Canadian clergyman and his wife, the Reverend and Mrs. R. W. Hardy, had been visiting the Maritime Museum during its regular hours. While taking the tour through the Queen's House, they were so impressed with the stately beauty of the Tulip Staircase that they decided to photograph it. Mr. Hardy stood ready with his camera, but had to wait for several minutes until it was clear of tourists and people working in the building. But Reverend Hardy was a patient man, and before long the moment arrived. The staircase was deserted, and he snapped his picture of it.

When the Hardys returned to Canada, the clergyman had the roll of film developed at a local shop. When the pictures were ready, the Hardys began looking through them. Coming across the one of the presumably vacant Tulip Staircase, they gazed at it in complete bewilderment. Two ghostly figures shrouded in white appeared distinctly upon the print. One of the cowled phantoms was climbing the staircase with his left hand on the railing. The hand had a large ring on one of its fingers. Just ahead of this figure was another that was less clear, but with a hand also grasping the railing.

Neither Reverend Hardy nor his wife had ever had much interest in ghosts or psychic matters; indeed, they had never believed in such things. However, they could not deny the existence of the eerie phantoms in their photograph. They both thought they should report the occurrence to someone, but who? Finally, the Hardys decided to send the picture to The Ghost Club, a famous London organization founded in 1862 which investigates hauntings and other occult phenomena.

In London, authorities at The Ghost Club were much intrigued by the clergyman's remarkable photograph. Immediately the club began a thorough investigation both of the story and the picture. The photo was submitted to experts at the Kodak Company who testified that no manipulation of the actual film could have occurred. Furthermore, officials at the Queen's House corroborated the Hardys' story that there had been nobody on the staircase when the picture was snapped, and also that Reverend Hardy had taken the photo during daylight hours.

The only logical conclusion Ghost Club researchers could reach was that two persons, or apparitions of them, had been on the stairs at the instant Reverend Hardy had exposed his film. In 1967 the Hardys again visited England. At this time they were questioned exhaustively by an official of The Ghost Club, whose judgment was that the clergyman and his wife were people of the highest integrity and incapable of fraud or trickery.

At a later date, arrangements were made for members of The Ghost Club to conduct an all-night "ghost watch" at the Queen's House. All of their latest equipment for investigating psychic phenomena was brought into play. Controls were set up in strategic locations around the Tulip Staircase for recording atmospheric conditions, with thermometer readings being taken every few minutes. Sensitive sound-recording devices were activated to run continuously. Still cameras using both standard and infra-red film were set up to cover all angles of the staircase. Movie cameras were set rolling. Delicate instruments were set up to show drafts and vibrations, and the stair rail was coated with petroleum jelly and later checked for fingerprints.

During their vigil that night, Club investigators tried to "tempt" the ghosts by remaining silent for long periods and plunging the Queen's House into total darkness. Communication with the alleged spirits was also attempted by automatic writing, Ouija board, and table-tipping. But these endeavors failed to turn up anything.

Nevertheless, The Ghost Club did get some results that night. Among these were the recorded sounds of muttering, footsteps, and weeping. Once there was also the thin peal of a bell, which was heard by all present. But when the Ghost Club investigators developed their films, they found nothing of a phantasmal nature on them. So the enigma of the Hardys' remarkable photograph remains unsolved. If it is genuine—and most investigators believe it is—it is probably one of the best spontaneous ghost photographs ever made.

In the investigation of this apparition case, the time factor may have been a significant one. Some haunting apparitions manifest themselves only at certain times. The Ghost Club conducted their vigil during nighttime hours, while Reverend Hardy had snapped his picture in the afternoon during daylight. Just possibly, the shrouded figures caught on the clergyman's film may have been daytime haunters.

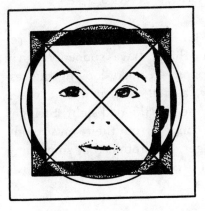

"LARRY," THE EASTER POLTERGEIST

POLTERGEISTS THAT MANIFEST THEMSELVES AS MAN-SIZED vibrating columns of fluorescent light are comparatively rare in psychic literature. Probably the best known was the one that began to disturb the home of Graham Stringer in 1958. Furthermore, this ghost brought with it a new twist in the timing of its appearances: it was in the habit of coming at Eastertime.

The Stringers and their four-year-old son lived on Trafalgar Avenue in the Peckham section of London. The ghost received no publicity the first year it appeared because the Stringers tried to keep the matter quiet. But the following year, psychical researchers were called in to try to find some explanation for the occurrences.

"It was on Good Friday," Graham Stringer later told reporters, "that we first saw the thing." It was suddenly seen in the vicinity of their living room—a milky-looking fluorescent cylinder-shaped entity, as tall as a man of average height. A few seconds after seeing the odd sight, Stringer and his wife smelled smoke coming from their son's room.

"There," continued Stringer, "we found that something had burned a hole through the center of a pile of the baby's

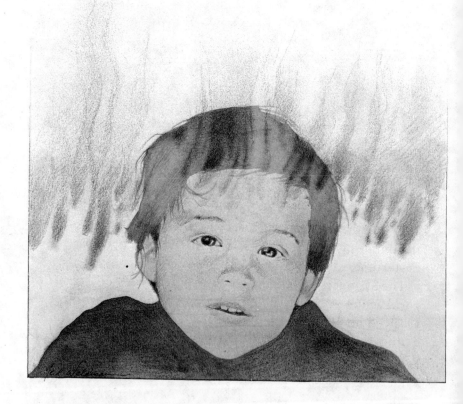

clothes. It looked just as though a blowtorch had done it. Yet
a pair of nylons on the bottom of the pile was untouched—
and you know how flammable they are."

Evidently the little boy had seen the ghost, too, for he kept
asking his parents what the thing had been. Finally, he
pestered them so long with his questions that Stringer and
his wife thought it would be a good idea to give the ghost a
name. So they decided to call him Larry.

"You see," Stringer told a reporter from United Press
International, "we had to give the child some sort of explanation. We didn't want to frighten him with a lot of ghost talk."

Throughout the rest of 1958 and into early spring of 1959,
"Larry" remained relatively quiet. Sometimes an object
would be tossed about or articles were heard to drop or a
faint thumping would be heard—that was all. But when the
Easter season rolled around again, the vibrating column of
light was seen a second time.

When Graham Stringer had a pair of shoes yanked brutally out of his hands, he decided his family could use some
expert help. He contacted the British College of Psychic
Science, a much-respected research organization. A small
team of investigators did all they could to induce Larry to
appear to them, but had little success except for minor disturbances such as hearing thumpings and other noises.
However, they experienced enough activity to label the disturbances as poltergeistic in nature.

In addition, the psychic researchers subjected Mr. and
Mrs. Stringer to exhaustive questioning. From Stringer's
wife, they elicited the information that, as an adolescent, she
had indeed undergone poltergeist experiences, although
they were not of a severe nature. These included odd knockings and items around the house being inexplicably dropped
or misplaced in some way. Under similar questioning, Mr.

Stringer recalled that during their honeymoon, incidents of a similar nature had occurred, although the couple had not paid much attention to them.

By now the Stringers had caught on to the annual appearence of Larry, and when Easter of 1960 approached, they wondered what would happen next. Nervously they waited, fearing another conflagration. It came soon enough. Again the awesome column of vibrating light energy appeared, and they were powerless to prevent the ghost from once again setting fire to and destroying another bundle of clothing.

Then, apparently not content with this demonstration, Larry prolonged his visit at the Stringer house. Among other activities, clocks were shifted about on the mantelpiece, and crockery, knickknacks, and other items were seen by the family to sail about the apartment. These occurrences continued for several days after Easter Sunday. Graham Stringer, then a free-lance photographer, said that Larry once put on a demonstration in his darkroom. "The room lit up," he later told reporters. "And there was Larry vibrating at my side."

When Easter of 1961 approached and Larry was once again due to show up, the Stringers decided to try exorcism. They got in touch with a local Catholic priest and asked him if he would perform the rites at their apartment. The priest assented and came the next day, conducting the complete ceremony and blessing the Stringer home with holy water.

"It seemed to have done the trick," remarked Graham Stringer to reporters. "We congratulated ourselves all around."

For a year it did seem to work. However, it turned out that Larry had only taken a year's leave of absence. With the coming of the 1962 Easter season, the poltergeist struck again. The Stringers' living room furniture burst suddenly into flames and fire also destroyed a large carpet. Later their young son's bed spontaneously burst into flames.

A friend of Graham Stringer suggested that they contact a medium who might be able to shed some light on the disturbances. Accordingly the medium came to the apartment, looked around carefully, and then went into a short trance. Later, the medium revealed that Larry was the spirit of Mrs. Stringer's brother, Charles, who had died of severe burns some twenty years earlier at the age of a year and a half.

"Now that the spirit has made his identity known," the medium promised, "he will leave the family in peace."

And in fact the Easter poltergeist never did return to burn any more clothing or furniture in the Stringers' home. Furthermore, the medium's revelation provides a key to explaining the case. Conceivably, Larry may indeed have been the spirit of Charles; possibly his return was triggered by some long-repressed subconscious guilt on the part of Mrs. Stringer who may, as a child, have considered herself in some way to blame for her little brother's death.

THE
HAUNTED
EGYPTIAN
BONE

USUALLY POLTERGEIST ACTIVITY INVOLVES THE movement—tossing about, hurling, flight, or other disturbances—of an object or objects. But in this highly unusual case, a specific object itself—a pilfered bone from an ancient Egyptian skeleton—appears to have been the focal cause of some very violent poltergeist events. Moreover, the haunted Egyptian bone seems to have brought about the appearance of some apparitions as well. And there is also the possibility that a mysterious Egyptian curse was connected with the case.

The people in the case were Sir Alexander Hay Seton, the tenth Baronet of Abercorn, and his wife, Zeyla. In 1936 Sir Alexander and Zeyla were visiting Egypt, and it was here

that their strange story began. They made the regular tourist treks to the tomb of Tutankhamen, the Temple at Luxor,
and other historic and ancient sites. One day they visited the
Valley of the Kings on camelback, and Sir Alexander described the animals later as "rather unpleasant." They were,
however, staying at one of the finest hotels in Cairo, close to
Gizeh where the Sphinx and the Great Pyramids lay, and
they thoroughly enjoyed the excellent cuisine and bathing
there.

During their stay in Cairo, they met a local guide named
Abdul who offered to take them around to some unusual
places which most tourists never saw. He said he could take
the Setons to visit a tomb that had just been opened and was
being excavated by archeologists. This sounded like a fine
opportunity to Sir Alexander and Zeyla, and they told Abdul
to arrange the tour as soon as he could.

When the day arrived, Abdul conducted the Setons to the
tomb and led them down some two dozen steps hewn out of
solid rock and into the tomb's main chamber. There, on a
stone slab, lay a mouldering skeleton amid scraps and twists
of winding cloth that had rotted away over the centuries.
Abdul told Sir Alexander that she had been a girl of the
upper classes, one of many whose remains had been found in
the Gizeh area. When the Setons had inspected the contents
of the tomb, they and their guide ascended into the sunlight
again. Zeyla, however, had been so fascinated by the tomb
that she stole back down for a last look by herself. She did not
stay long, and soon she, her husband, and Abdul were on
their way back to Cairo.

Back at the hotel that evening, Lady Seton confessed to Sir
Alexander that she had taken something from the tomb's
chamber. She held out her hand, and in it lay a strange-
looking bone. It had belonged to the skeleton of the girl on

the slab. "It looked," wrote Sir Alexander in an unpublished manuscript, "like a digestive biscuit, slightly convex and shaped like a heart." It was, in fact, the skeleton's sacrum, the last bone on the vertebral column that is attached to the pelvis.

When the Setons returned to their home in Edinburgh, they invited some friends in one evening to tell them about their trip to Egypt. Sir Alexander then displayed to his guests the bone that Zeyla had taken from the tomb. After everyone had examined it, Seton, with a feigned ceremonial dignity, placed it gingerly in a glass display case that he put temporarily on a small table in the dining room. A couple of hours later, just as their guests were leaving, the poltergeist activity commenced. Outside, under the portico of the house, Sir Alexander was bidding his friends good-bye when a large chunk of roof parapet crashed to the ground just inches from where he was standing. The following morning, Seton found that a chimney pot had fallen to the ground. From that time on, a series of such calamitous incidents began, and Sir Alexander, connecting them to the stolen bone, came to believe that he and his wife were under the spell of an Egyptian curse.

About a week later, the Setons' children's nanny burst into their bedroom and blurted out that she was sure she had heard someone or something moving about in the dining room. Seton hurried downstairs for a look around. He found nothing to account for the sounds and nothing seemed to be out of place. That same night, a couple of hours later, he himself heard a heavy thud that sounded as if it had come from the direction of the dining room. Next morning, Zeyla accused him of upsetting the table on which the glass case containing the bone had been resting. On the floor lay the open case and the bone which had rolled out of it. Sir Alex-

ander denied having upset the case, but thought it possible that he might have placed the table unevenly against the wall; perhaps vibrations from the heavy traffic outside the town house had caused it to topple over.

In the ensuing weeks, many more baffling crashes and other sounds were heard in the Setons' Edinburgh town house. Then people began seeing apparitions. A young nephew of Sir Alexander's was the first to witness one. The young man had come to stay for a few days, and one morning he reported that when he had gone to the downstairs lavatory during the night he had observed a "funny-dressed person going up the stairs." Then the servants, too, claimed that they had seen a phantomlike robed figure roaming around the house at night. It was not long before the Setons had difficulty in keeping domestic help.

Meanwhile, Sir Alexander had shifted the case containing the bone from the dining room to the upstairs drawing room, where he kept his collection of valuable snuff-boxes. Convinced now that the hateful bone was the cause of his woes, he decided one night to keep watch over it. Locking all the doors and windows, he took up a position on the balcony outside the drawing room. Nothing untoward happened for several hours, so Seton decided to give up and go to bed. He took the key to the locked drawing room with him to his room. A short while later, he was awakened by his wife, who had heard noises coming from the locked room containing the bone.

Immediately, Sir Alexander grabbed his revolver and made for the drawing room. On his way he encountered a badly frightened nanny who had also heard noises issuing from the locked room. When Seton unlocked the room, he found it looking, in his own words, "as if a battle royal had taken place." Books were strewn about, furniture had been moved, chairs were upside down, a vase was upset. Yet in the middle of this colossal mess sat the Egyptian bone—serenely untouched. Checking the windows, he found them all still tightly locked, and there appeared to be no possible way that anybody could have entered the room.

After this episode, the Setons enjoyed a few weeks of peace and quiet. Then, just as they thought the "curse" had been lifted from them, the bangings, crashes, thuds, and other weird sounds began again—and always they appeared to come from the drawing room. After a few days of this discomfort, Sir Alexander and his wife decided to leave only the heavy furniture in the drawing room and shift all of the articles that had been tossed about to their downstairs sitting room. The glass case containing the bone, together with the table on which it rested, was also taken downstairs.

Barely a week later, the Setons returned to their house to find the sitting room in an unbelievable state of disarray. Chairs and tables had been tipped over, books were scattered all about, glassware and ornaments were smashed—no article at all seemed to be in its accustomed place. While one of the legs of the table on which the glass case rested had been cracked, the case and the bone remained untouched.

Inevitably, the newspapers got hold of the story, and soon there were glaring headlines not only in the Edinburgh editions, but also in other Scottish papers. One read: BARONET FEARS PHARAOH CURSE ON FAMILY. One reporter got permission to borrow the bone for a few days; he returned it at the end of a week, saying that nothing unusual had taken place. Two weeks later, he became ill and had to have emergency surgery on his abdomen.

Not long after this, Sir Alexander and his wife left their town house in Edinburgh. Seton himself remarked that he thought their nerves were frayed because of the strange goings-on. At any rate, the couple had a serious quarrel, and they decided to live apart temporarily. Zeyla took her five-year-old daughter and left Edinburgh to stay with her family. Seton took up quarters at his club. Before he did so, however, he moved the glass case with the bone in it back upstairs to the drawing room.

Left alone now in the house was the loyal old nanny. One night not long after her employers had moved out, she heard a resounding crash. It had come from the vicinity of the drawing room upstairs. But the woman was too petrified to go up there. When she told Sir Alexander about it, the Baronet went up to investigate, but he found the chamber quite undisturbed—except for the Egyptian bone and the table on which it had rested. Seton found the table sprawled on its side and completely broken. Beside its wreckage lay the bone—split into five pieces.

The press, continuing to follow the story, was filled with suggestions as to what the Setons ought to do about the bone with the "curse" on it. One was that they should get rid of the bone altogether. Lady Seton, however, absolutely refused to do this. Another story alleged that Sir Alexander had made plans to send Lady Seton back to Egypt to return the bone to its rightful place in the tomb at Gizeh. Among other suggestions was one that the bone be thrown into the sea; another was that it be buried. Meanwhile, Seton got many offers from people who wanted to buy the bone; however, he rejected all of these, for he did not want others to suffer from the "curse." Next, Lady Seton took the five pieces of the bone to a physician and requested that he cement them back into one piece again. This was done, and the bone was now put on a table in the hallway next to the dining room. A newspaper story about this time reported that a maid working for the doctor who had mended the bone broke her leg while running in panic from a gliding robed figure she had seen while the bone was being worked on.

Not long after the bone had been repaired, Sir Alexander and his wife—who did occasionally meet socially—gave a dinner party for some guests. When the festivities were at their height, the bone together with the table it sat on suddenly took off across the hall and smashed into the opposite wall with a great crash. No one had been near the bone at the time, but the unnerving event caused two women to faint, and the Setons' guests soon left in consternation.

Following this occurrence, Seton made up his mind that he must get rid of the bone once and for all. This, he thought, would best be done by destroying it. He and Zeyla were back together again temporarily; however, Seton knew his wife would not agree to the destruction of the bone, so he waited until she left the house for a few days. As an added precaution, he arranged for his uncle, a minister from a nearby abbey, to come and exorcise whatever evil spirit the bone might contain. After these rites were performed, Seton, the faithful nanny, and Seton's uncle proceeded to destroy the relic. The nanny later confirmed its end: "He brought it into the kitchen, and we put it on the fire and watched it burn. It took a long time, and what was left we put into a bucket with the ashes."

Seton later wrote in his unpublished manuscript, "The curse did not end with the destruction of the bone. From 1936 onwards trouble always seemed to beset me. Zeyla never forgave me for destroying the bone, and it did not help our already rocky marriage."

And, in fact, the couple were divorced in mid-1939. Although Zeyla remarried, she experienced ill health and much misfortune and died a few years later. Sir Alexander remarried in 1939, but the couple separated in 1953, then divorced five years later. In 1962 he took a third wife. This Lady Seton later remarked that her husband was outwardly perpetually cheerful; inwardly, however, he was a depressed man. She said that he often talked of the bone and firmly believed that it had had a baleful effect on his existence. "I was born during an earthquake," he wrote in his manuscript, "and my life has been a tremor ever since."

Sir Alexander's third marriage was a short one. On his

honeymoon, he told his wife that he had a premonition that they would be married for only six months. In fact, he died seven months later, still convinced that the pilfered relic from the Egyptian tomb had brought about the bad luck in his life.

The mystery of just how the mouldering bone produced the poltergeist activity, and presumably the robed apparitions as well, remains an enigma. Few if any theories in psychical research can account for the phenomena in this case. Somehow, perhaps, the spirit of the Egyptian girl of long ago—outraged at having had her skeleton violated— may have been able to induce great power to act through the bone, using it as a talisman to work violent damage in the Setons' home.

THE GHOSTS OF VERSAILLES

ONE OF THE MOST FAMOUS OF ALL APPARITION CASES happened to two English school principals on a holiday in France. Their strange experiences occurred on a Saturday afternoon, August 10, 1901, in the Petit Trianon gardens at Versailles, just outside Paris. Fascinated by what had happened to them, the two women later published a book called simply *An Adventure* about the odd occurrences on that afternoon. It became an immediate best-seller, and thousands of people read it.

The two Englishwomen were Miss Anne Moberly and Miss Eleanor Jourdain, and they had taken rooms in Paris for their short vacation. On their list of places to visit was the Palace of Versailles, with its gardens built for King Louis XIV

19

in the mid-1600s. Arriving that Saturday shortly after noon, the two friends started out on their famous walk through the grounds. Neither had seen Versailles before. After a few minutes, they reached the palace of the Grand Trianon. Then, instead of taking the customary tourist route along the main road, they decided to stroll down the shady sunken land to the right of the Grand Trianon forecourt. A short while later, they arrived at the gardener's gate on the grounds of the Petit Trianon.

In their book, the two women admitted they weren't exactly sure at what point their adventure actually began. It may have been at the corner of the sunken lane where Miss Moberly saw a woman dressed in peculiar-looking clothes and shaking a white cloth out of a window in a nearby house. At any rate, they continued up the lane and turned right past some buildings. They peered into one of them but did not go in.

Presently, the women had their choice of three paths to follow. They chose the middle one because on it, a little way ahead, they saw two men, and they wanted to ask directions of them. At the time, they assumed the men were gardeners, because not far from them stood a wheelbarrow with a spade in it. Some time after their experiences, Miss Moberly thought it possible that they weren't gardeners at all, but officials of some kind. One man was older than the other, and both were clad in long gray-green coats and wore three-cornered hats. Also, both had in their hands what might have been ceremonial staffs. Reaching them, Miss Jourdain asked directions. Both men replied in an odd mechanical fashion to continue straight along the path they had been following.

At this juncture, off to the right, Miss Jourdain happened to see a sturdy stone house. Standing in the doorway were a woman and a girl dressed in unusual clothes. Each wore a kerchief tucked into her bodice, and the girl's long dress reached to her ankles. The woman was just handing a jug to the girl.

As they continued on their walk, a strange feeling suddenly came over the two friends. Miss Moberly later described it as "an extraordinary depression . . . which, in spite of every effort, steadily deepened." She also described the sur-

rounding trees as appearing flat and lifeless, "like a woods worked in tapestry." Miss Jourdain later wrote, "There was a feeling of depression about the place. I began to feel as if I were walking in my sleep; the heavy dreariness was oppressive."

Not long after this, the two women reached a point where the path ended. Before them they saw a small clump of trees within which stood a garden kiosk; it was circular and resembled a small bandstand. Sitting by the kiosk was a sinister-looking dark-complexioned man. He was wearing a long cloak and a large three-cornered hat. His face was marked by smallpox, and his dour expression alarmed the women.

At that moment, they heard someone running up toward them in breathless haste. It was another man, who had apparently just come over a large rock at the point where the path ended. The Englishwomen were shocked and frightened by his appearance. In Miss Moberly's words, he was "distinctly a gentleman, tall, with large eyes, and the effect of the crisp, curling black hair under a large sombrero hat was to make him look like an old picture." He wore buckled shoes and a large cloak. The man looked greatly excited as he stopped and called to the two women in French, "Mesdames, mesdames, do not go that way!" Then he waved his arms wildly and called again, "Go this way!" The petrified women watched in wonder as he ran off again with a curious smile on his face.

The running man had indicated to the women that they should go to the right, which they were only too willing to do for it led them away from the evil-looking man near the kiosk. They crossed over a small rustic bridge and followed a narrow path under trees until they eventually came to the Petit Trianon.

In reality, the two friends had arrived at the north side of the famous chateau instead of the main entrance, and they were in what was called the English Garden. Walking around to the west side of the stately house, they found themselves on the terrace and there Miss Moberly saw a lady, seated on the grass with her back to them, sketching. She wore a floppy white hat perched on masses of fair hair and a long-waisted, full-skirted summer dress with a kerchief over her bodice and around her shoulders. The sketching lady turned and saw them, looking full at them as they passed by.

Only later did Miss Moberly discover that her friend had been distracted and had not herself seen the sketching figure. At any rate, after much research and reflection on their strange experience, the two women came to the conclusion that this was none other than the apparition of Queen Marie Antoinette of France, as she appeared in the year 1789. The queen of the doomed King Louis XVI would then have been thirty-four, and only four years away from her own death on the guillotine during the French Revolution. Miss Moberly later wrote that, "It was not a young face, and though rather pretty it did not attract me."

Next, the two women went up the steps from the terrace and Miss Moberly again saw the sketching lady, this time from behind, and noticed that her three-cornered kerchief was pale green. Crossing the entrance, the friends looked over into the walled courtyard that formed the main entrance to the Petit Trianon.

Puzzled as to how to get around to the main entrance, the friends wandered into what is known as the French Garden. Just as they did so, a door of an outbuilding opened, and a young man in the attire of a footman stepped jauntily outside. He called to them and offered to show them the way around to the main entrance. The young man gave them

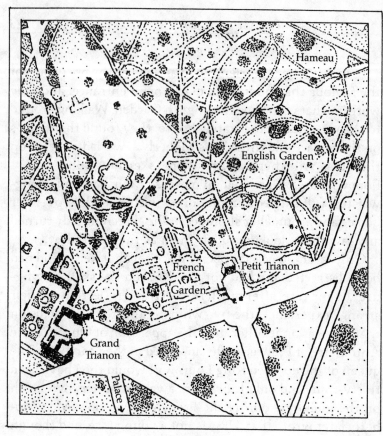

VERSAILLES

directions in French, which the two Englishwomen understood. They followed these directions and soon lost sight of the man.

While passing through the French Garden, Miss Moberly later wrote that "the feeling of depression was very strong here." When at length they reached the front entrance of the Petit Trianon, they both had the distinct feeling that they were now back in the real world of 1901. They drove back to their hotel in Paris, thoroughly mystified by their odd experience.

In fact, this was the only such extraordinary experience

Miss Moberly had in the Trianon gardens. Miss Jourdain, however, was to have two more in the next seven years, each when she was alone. The first of these occurred on January 2, 1902, when she went for the second time to Versailles. She did not retrace her old route but went along a path leading to a section of the gardens known as the Hameau. For a while she felt none of the eerie depressed feeling she had had the previous August. "But," she wrote later, "on crossing a bridge to go to the Hameau, the old feeling returned in full force; it was as if I had crossed a special line and was suddenly in a circle of influence."

As she walked in the Hameau, Miss Jourdain saw a cart being filled with sticks by two laborers who wore tunics and capes with pointed hoods. Returning from the Hameau, she took a wrong turn and found herself in a dense clump of trees. Here she heard faint music, as if played by a far-off band, and she also had the distinct impression that people in rustling silk dresses were all around her. When she finally found her way back to the main gardens of Versailles, she inquired and was told that no band or orchestra had played anywhere in the vicinity that day.

Miss Jourdain visited Versailles several times in the next few years, without any repetition of these events. Her next and last strange experience in the gardens of Versailles took place on September 12, 1908. On that day nothing happened until the last hour or so of her visit. Then, in passing the Corps of Guards building, she saw two women in old-fashioned costumes sitting in the shade near a gate. They were arguing in loud voices.

"It felt," she wrote later, "as though I were being taken up into another condition of things quite as real as the former. The women's voices, though their quarrel was just as shrill and eager as before, seemed to be fading away so quickly that they would soon be altogether gone; from their tones the dispute was clearly going on still, but seemed to have less and less power to reach me.

"I turned at once to look back and saw the gates near which they were sitting melting away, and the background of trees again becoming visible through them, as on our original visit, but I noticed that the side pillars were standing steady. The whole scene—sky, trees, and buildings—gave a little shiver, like the movement of a curtain or of scenery at the theater. At the same time, the old difficulty of walking on and of making any headway reproduced itself, together with the feeling of depression described in 1901 and 1902.

"But I instantly decided to keep to my plan of going straight out by the lane, and, once outside the lane, things became natural again. Yet the sudden startling sense of insecurity left a deep impression, so little did I expect any repetition of the old phenomena after the innumerable un-eventful visits I had paid to the Trianon since the winter of 1902."

Apart from these experiences—and of course the original one in 1901—nothing further of a supernatural nature happened to either of the women. Still, their initial experience together continued to fascinate them, and they spent the next ten years searching through documents, trying to identify each detail of the occurrence. Every bit of corroborating evidence was carefully deposited in the Bodleian Library at Oxford. The friends retraced their steps in the gardens of Versailles many times, both together and individually. Everything was checked—location of trees and shrubs, dress of the court and of ordinary people, architecture of the day—hundreds of minute details. The culmination of it all was the publication of their book in 1911, which created an immediate sensation.

In *An Adventure*, the Misses Moberly and Jourdain had concluded that in the course of their first experience they had seen the Petit Trianon as it had been in 1789. Their reasoning was that August 10, the date of their visit, was a significant one because it was on that date in 1792—three years later—that the Tuileries Palace in Paris was sacked by mobs during the bloody French Revolution. Early that morning, the royal family had managed to escape to the Hall of Assembly. Miss Moberly and Miss Jourdain's theory was that they had somehow inadvertently "entered within an act of the queen's memory when she was still alive." That is, the queen, shut up in the Hall of Assembly as a prisoner, had gone back in her memory to other Augusts spent in the Trianon chateau. The last of these was 1789—the year of the outbreak of the French Revolution—and it was the two friends' hypothesis that in some unexplained way they had stepped backward in time to that happier August 10 in Queen Marie Antoinette's life. The sketching lady, they believed, was Marie Antoinette herself, and into the framework of the picture they strove through intense research to fit other events and characters of the drama they witnessed.

Many readers of *An Adventure*, of course, believed that the whole business was a figment of the authors' imaginations. Yet it turned out that other visitors to the gardens of Versailles have had similar experiences. These observers have felt the same tension in the atmosphere near the Trianon, the same unaccountable depression, and have caught glimpses of shadowy figures of people in the clothing of a previous era.

For instance, on an October afternoon in 1928, two other Englishwomen, Miss Burrow and Miss Lambert, also witnessed a series of strange occurrences in the Versailles gardens. Neither had heard of *An Adventure* at the time of their visit, and so could not have formed preconceived ideas of what they might encounter there. These ladies, instead of going down the main walk to the Petit Trianon's front entrance after leaving the Grand Trianon, walked to the left, passed the farm buildings, and entered the garden by the gardeners' entrance. It was exactly here that the Misses Moberly and Jourdain had met the two gardeners (or officials with staffs) dressed in green.

Later Miss Burrow related how they first came upon a deserted building hemmed in by a briar patch, and that here an eerie feeling of oppression suddenly came over her. Miss Lambert added that the same thing happened to her. The two stopped talking and hastened on until they came in sight of the ruined farm buildings near the gardeners' gate. From the window of a stone farmhouse there, they could see a woman looking down on them. She was wearing a high muslin cap.

Upon turning to look for one of the chateaus through the trees, the Misses Lambert and Burrow saw an old man whom they judged to be an official of some kind approaching down a side lane. He seemed over sixty years old, and the livery he was dressed in included silver braid, large cuffs, white stockings, buckled shoes, and a stick with a knob and a tassel. He was wearing a three-cornered hat with a high turned-up brim. Later, Miss Burrow, when questioned by a member of the French Society for Psychical Research, drew a sketch of the man. It revealed that he was wearing a *roquelaure*, a kind of overcoat with multiple collars and large cuffs, worn in the period between 1773 and 1800.

At the time of her experience, Miss Burrow called to the man, wishing to ask him where the Petit Trianon was located. She heard him shout back at her in a strange form of French dialect. She later wrote that he answered by shouting "sentence after sentence in hoarse unintelligible French as if in great haste." Something about his face seemed so hostile and strange that the two women hurried on their way. Looking over their shoulders a few seconds later, they saw that he had completely vanished.

The sketching lady—presumably Queen Marie Antoinette—has also been seen by visitors to the Versailles gardens. All three members of one family saw her not once but twice. Both times she was dressed in a light cream-colored skirt and a white floppy hat. Both times, as she was busily sketching, she was seen to hold out a paper at some distance from her, as though judging its artistic merits. One of the observers, who at the same time complained that he was almost overcome by terrible fatigue, commented, "All the contours of her figure and her general bearing were not what we are accustomed to now. Not only was her dress out-of-date, but she herself belonged to another century."

While the case still remains a mystery today, it was one of the rarest types in psychical research; namely, *retrocognition*, which is knowledge of the past or past events acquired by apparently paranormal means. The noted British researcher G. N. M. Tyrell wrote of the case, "So far as their finding themselves surrounded by a complete hallucinatory environment is concerned, there is no need even to go to the supernormal for a precedent. The resources of the personality are equal to providing it. The difficulty, of course, is to explain how their environment came to correspond to the gardens as they were in 1789."

THE
SPECTER
OF
U-BOAT 65

ONE OF THE MOST VIOLENT OF ALL APPARITION CASES concerned a German submarine roaming the seas during World War I. Even while she was being built, U-Boat 65 seemed unlucky—jinxed from the moment her keel was laid. During her construction, three men died from inhaling engine-room fumes, and two others were crushed by a steel girder which suddenly fell from its slings. When she was finally finished in 1915, U-Boat 65 was—for that day—modern, sleek, and trim. But soon her crew came to hate her.

On the very first day of her sea trials, an officer making a routine inspection of her hull was seen to walk deliberately overboard. He was never seen again. On the U-Boat's maiden dive, she refused to respond to her surfacing mechanism, and for fourteen hours she lay on the ocean floor as crewmen labored frantically to repair her waterlogged batteries. At last, reluctantly, she wallowed to the surface. As other strange incidents occurred aboard the sub, sailors began to petition for transfers to another ship. Several wound up in naval prisons because they refused to return aboard the sub after their leaves were up. Then, late in 1915, occurred the most tragic incident to date. When the U-65 was taking on supplies at dockside on the Belgian coast at Bruges, a torpedo blew up while being maneuvered into a firing tube. Six men were killed—the U-65's first lieutenant and five petty officers.

It was on a September morning in 1916 that the apparition was first seen. The U-65 had been at sea in the English Channel, preying on Allied shipping, and now she needed to surface and recharge her batteries. As the lean, sharklike hull emerged dripping from the gray waters, the captain was at his periscope and two lookouts were stationed at observation hatches. All three of them saw the astonishing sight quite clearly: a man was standing motionless, his arms folded, on the submarine's bow.

"It's the first lieutenant," shrieked one of the lookouts, breaking the silence. "He's come back! He's standing there!"

The second time the ghost was seen was in November 1916. The U-65 was in drydock at Bruges, where she had been ordered for repairs by Admiral von Schroeder of the German High Command. The crew was given leave and only a skeleton watch was left aboard the submarine. The following night, the petty officer of the watch, wildly excited and clearly frightened, burst into the Officer of the Deck's cabin and shouted, "I saw it, sir! It's come on board—the ghost of the first lieutenant. Pederson saw it, too! He was standing in the bows with his arms folded!"

"Are you sure?" questioned the officer.

"As sure as I see you sitting there, sir," the man replied. "Pederson can confirm it."

Although the incident was reported to the High Command, the admirals thought it best to hush up the affair. They had had troubles enough with the unlucky ship as it was. Besides, they told each other, it was probably due to battle fatigue on the part of nervous, frightened crewmen.

When everyone was back from leave, the U-65 was sent out again to harass the Allied shipping lanes. This time everything went well, and during the second week in December, the sub torpedoed and sank an enemy merchantman. The crew began to think that their ship was no longer jinxed. Morale began to improve.

But then the ghost was seen again. One morning early in January 1917, shortly after the torpedoing of the Allied merchantman, the U-65 surfaced to recharge her batteries. Once again the terrified lookouts saw the apparition in the bows.

Crewmen passed the word swiftly throughout the whole ship. "It's come back again! It's standing there with its arms folded!"

The captain, realizing he must do something to break the evil spell cast on his ship, threw open the conning tower hatch. Cupping his hands to his mouth, he shouted, "You there! Who are you?"

Very slowly, reported several witnesses, the phantom in the bows turned its head toward the captain. Its face was that of the dead lieutenant. Abruptly the captain slammed the hatch shut again and gave orders to dive the ship. But apparently the ghost was still with them, for the crew could hear soft laughter echoing through the submarine for several minutes.

Even the captain was thoroughly shaken now, and he pointed the U-65 back toward its home port of Bruges. As they were docking there, an Allied bombing of the port was in progress. Suddenly, as the captain stood in the conning tower, a shell fragment pierced it, killing him instantly.

When the High Command learned of these latest developments aboard the U-65, it had little choice but to take action. Admiral von Schroeder ordered the jinxed vessel to be docked indefinitely and the crew to be given compassionate leave. Then he ordered a navy chaplain to conduct a service of exorcism. It was hoped that these rites would rid the ship of the ghost forever.

But it appeared that the apparition had other plans. Late in 1917, because it was needed to patrol the English Channel, the U-65 was again sent to sea. In the last year of the war, during May 1918, off Cape Finisterre, more peculiar events happened aboard the U-65. Three crewmen—all of whom had claimed to see the ghost of the dead lieutenant—died in strange ways. A gunner's mate seemed to go mad one afternoon and went below and killed himself. That night a man in the engine room caught a sudden fever and died during the early morning hours. Later that day, a young petty officer flung himself overboard to his death.

When the submarine returned to Bruges and the High Command heard of these events, the entire crew of the U-65 was reassigned, a new crew was brought aboard, and the ship was completely overhauled in drydock. In mid-June 1918, under a new commanding officer, the U-65 was again ordered to sea duty.

So the submarine slipped her lines, with batteries freshly recharged, and proceeded out into the Atlantic sea lanes. Her orders were to prowl off the Irish coast and seek out convoys to attack. But the German Naval High Command had seen

the last of the U-65, for she never returned from this tour of duty. Evidently the troublesome apparition was still aboard and was continuing to disrupt the crew. But just what happened to the ill-fated ship was never to be known.

On the morning of July 10, 1918, the United States submarine L-2, on patrol off the Irish coast, spotted what looked like a U-boat on the horizon. As the L-2 approached cautiously, her captain could see that it *was* an enemy submarine; her hull number was U-65. The American captain was puzzled. There seemed to be no sign of life aboard the sub and she was simply drifting, as if she were a derelict.

The L-2 closed in toward the U-65 but, before the American captain could fire a warning salvo, a terrific explosion momentarily blotted out the German craft. The U-65 was then seen to rear up by the bows and then slide down into the gray seas again. The Americans could see she was sinking fast.

The American captain and two of his officers were watching intently through their binoculars, and all three men caught sight of a figure standing motionless in the bows of the sinking enemy sub. His arms were folded across his chest and he was seen to be smiling.

As a multiple-witness case, the U-65 affair is unique in the literature of psychical research. Seldom has an apparition been observed by so many independent witnesses and over such a long period of time—practically the whole four-year duration of World War I.

THE WHITE LADY OF KINSALE FORT

ONE OF THE BEST APPARITION CASES OF THIS OR ANY CEN-
tury involves the specter that continues to haunt Kinsale
Fort in County Cork, Ireland. A fine example of military
architecture, the old fort was constructed about the year
1678, and its battlements face out toward St. George's
Channel, where the American liner *Lusitania* was sunk in
1915. Kinsale itself, the tiny port in which the fort is situated, is a quaint town of old houses and narrow streets. In
one of its churchyards are buried three drowned passengers
of the *Lusitania*, including an unidentified woman. Some Kinsale residents are persuaded that the ghost that haunts Kinsale Fort is this unknown woman. But most agree that the
"White Lady," as she is known, is really the phantom of a

young bride who committed suicide on her wedding day over three hundred years ago.

There have been many observations of this ghost, especially by military personnel who have been stationed at the fort. Whenever the White Lady is seen, witnesses have reported that she fades from view almost as soon as they become aware that she is there. In the late 1870s, a Captain Hull and a brother officer were descending the fort's main staircase, when suddenly they stopped and stared at an eerie sight. On the small landing in front of them stood a young woman dressed in white. Both officers swore later that she had not been there a moment before. Although her face was beautiful, Hull said that it lacked color and had a peculiar corpselike pallor to it. As the two men continued to stare, the figure turned, gazed at them sorrowfully for a moment, and then vanished through a locked door.

A number of years prior to this incident, a Major Black had just been posted to a tour of duty at Kinsale Fort. One evening he was astonished to see a strange woman enter through the doorway of his quarters and walk up the stairs. At first Black thought she must be another officer's wife who had mistakenly come into the wrong apartment. He thought it queer that she made absolutely no sound as she ascended the stairs. Black also noticed that she was dressed all in white, and the style of her gown was distinctly old-fashioned. The major, fascinated, followed the white-clad figure upstairs and watched her enter one of the bedrooms. Seconds later he was in the bedroom himself, but the lady in white had mysteriously vanished.

A few weeks later, Major Black was planning to go away on a short trip. Two of his men were packing up some equipment to take with him, and his little daughter was watching them. Suddenly the girl asked the men, "Who is

that white lady bending over the banister and looking down on us?" The two soldiers looked up and could see nobody. Nevertheless, the major's daughter kept insisting that she had seen what she had seen—a young lady smiling down at her over the banister, dressed all in white.

There has also been violence connected with the White

Lady's apparition. In the fall of 1922, the fort's medical officer had just returned from several hours of snipe-shooting. Hearing the bugler blowing the call for mess, the doctor hurried toward his quarters to change into evening uniform. But he never made it to that particular meal. One of his fellow officers, noticing the doctor's absence, went to look for him and found him lying unconscious at the bottom of the stairs leading to his rooms.

When the doctor regained consciousness, he told a strange story. Just as he was bending down to get his key from under the doormat, he felt himself grabbed bodily from behind, dragged across the hall, and thrown violently down the stairs. As he fell, the doctor caught sight of a figure in a white dress. It looked, he said, like a young lady in a wedding gown.

Scarcely a year after this occurrence, a Captain Javes stationed at Kinsale Fort had a similar experience. One evening around dusk he was just about to enter his quarters when he heard queer rattling sounds coming from within. At that moment he caught a fleeting glimpse of a white-clad figure hurrying away from him down the hallway. Javes tried to open the door to his rooms, for he was curious to find out what the strange noises were. But it appeared to be locked from the inside; he could not budge it. Thinking that some friends were probably playing a practical joke on him, the captain shoved against the door with all his strength to force it open. As he did so, a cold draft of wind suddenly blew by him, and he felt himself being picked up by an unseen force and flung down the stairway. Like the doctor, Javes lay senseless for some time before being discovered by another officer.

On another occasion, a married officer and his wife were awakened one night by their children's nurse. She had been sleeping with the two children in a nearby chamber adjoining the apartment known as the White Lady's Room. The nurse had been unable to sleep and was simply lying in bed listening to the children's breathing when she saw a figure suddenly appear at the far corner of the room. The phantom was that of a young woman dressed in white, and it glided silently over to the bed in which the youngest child was sleeping. The figure gazed down at the little boy for a moment and then put its ghostly hand on his wrist. Instantly the boy awoke and screamed, "Take your cold hand away from my wrist!" Whereupon, the nurse told the parents, the specter promptly vanished.

The residents of Kinsale say that the incident that initiated the haunting took place just a few years after the fort was built. At that time a new military governor had taken up residence at the fort. This was Colonel Warrender, and he was known as a strict disciplinarian. The colonel had a daughter with the unusual name of Wilful, who married Sir Trevor Ashurst. On the still summer evening of their wedding day, the couple had gone for a stroll along the battlements of the fort. Presently the young bride exclaimed and pointed to some bizarre-looking flowers growing on the rocks below the fort. Just as Wilful expressed her wish to have the flowers, a sentry passed by. Smiling at the newlyweds, the soldier said he would be happy to climb down and pick them for her, provided Sir Trevor would take his place on guard while he did so.

Eager to please his bride, Sir Trevor agreed. He put on the sentry's jacket and took his rifle, while the soldier went to find some rope. Returning with several coils of stout line, he secured it to the parapet and lowered himself down from the battlements to the rocks below. Nearly an hour went by as Sir Trevor walked the sentry's post. Night was coming on and Wilful began to shiver in the cool air. Not wishing to desert the post, Sir Trevor sent his bride inside to their quarters. More time went by, and still the soldier did not return. The bridegroom, very tired after the events of the day, sat down with his back to the parapet and soon fell asleep.

Some minutes later, Colonel Warrender appeared. He was making one of his occasional personal inspections of the guard and challenged his son-in-law, whom he did not recognize in the darkness. But the bridegroom was fast asleep and did not answer the challenge. Seeing that the sentry was obviously asleep on duty, the colonel became infuriated, drew his pistol, and shot him through the heart. When he came closer and realized what he had done, the horrified Warrender sent for the surgeon. But it was too late. Sir Trevor was already dead.

A little while later Wilful learned what had happened to her husband. Distraught and hysterical, she rushed out of her bridal apartment and threw herself over the battlements to her death. On that night of horror, Colonel Warrender, upon learning of the second tragedy, took his own life.

In recent years, several visitors to Kinsale Fort have reported seeing the apparition of a young woman dressed in white. Most often it appears on still summer evenings, like the one so long ago when Wilful and Sir Trevor took their last stroll together.

For the sheer length of its duration alone—over three hundred years—the White Lady case would be a remarkable one. Yet it also has the rare combination of an apparition with tactile elements, such as observers feeling cold drafts and being touched and sometimes flung about by unknown forces. In the annals of psychic phenomena, the case of the White Lady of Kinsale Fort remains—to date, at least—an on-going one.

THE
CHICAGO
POLTERGEIST

FOR EVERY CASE OF POLTERGEIST ACTIVITY THAT IS reported to the police, psychic investigators, or other authorities, there are literally hundreds that are not. Understandably, the people involved fear the ridicule of friends, neighbors, and even the public at large. They also fear the possible loss of their jobs and being branded as queer or crazy. So they simply endure the often violent and destructive disturbances until they have run their course. In a very few of these cases, however, when sufficient time has gone by and children involved in the events have grown up and left home, the parent or parents in whose house or apartment the activity occurred will come forward.

One such case, which happened in the summer of 1974, came to light in 1980, although the woman who came forward asked that her real name not be used. The name given to her by the author of an article written about her was Mrs. Etta Jackson. She lived in a suburb of Chicago. One spring day in 1980 she happened to be reading the Sunday supplement of a local newspaper. The supplement contained a story about a poltergeist case that happened in another city; its author was a well-known writer on occult subjects. At the end of the article, the writer appealed to readers to contact him if they knew of any similar poltergeist cases. Etta Jackson got in touch with the writer and told him what had occurred in her apartment during August and September of 1974. She confided to the writer that she thought such "queer goings-on" ought to be "brought out in the open." Perhaps then, she added, they'd be better understood and "folks could maybe do something about them."

The first of the events, said Etta Jackson, happened in the early evening of August 12, 1974. She had been a widow since 1968 and lived in her small apartment with her two sons, Billy, aged 17, and Mark, aged 12. Arriving home from her job at a nearby electronics factory a little after 6 P.M., Mrs. Jackson, as she usually did during the hot months, went into the kitchen and made herself a tall glass of iced tea. Her two boys were in the living room watching TV, and she went in to join them. She had just settled down in an easy chair and was about to pick up the evening paper when the first odd thing happened. As her fingers curled to grasp the paper, it was suddenly snatched away, flew through the air, came apart as it did so, and landed in a jumbled heap across the room.

"Hey, Ma," Billy piped up, "how come you're throwing the newspaper around like that?"

"But I didn't do it," she protested.

A moment after that, the boys began to yell when the TV suddenly went off. Mark went to see if it had become unplugged, but it had not. And no amount of fiddling with the dials would make it come back on.

"I guess it needs a new tube or something," said Billy. "Gee, we were just getting into that movie, too."

Just as Billy finished saying this, a small circus began in the living room. A glass vase with some flowers in it toppled off the coffee table and spilled on the floor. Then they all saw Billy's outfielder's mitt, which had been resting on a chair, rise into the air, traverse the room, smack into the opposite wall, and fall to the floor. Next a stapler on the desk in the corner of the room slid off the desk and clattered to the floor below. As the woman and her sons watched speechless, they next saw Mark's math book, resting on the chair where the mitt had been, take off and crash into the coffee table.

"Hey, what's going on around here?" cried Mark. "Did you just see what I saw?"

"We all saw it," said Mrs. Jackson in a shaky voice.

"I think we got ourselves a ghost in here," whispered Billy, prophetically.

Then a crash was heard in the kitchen, and everybody rushed in to see what it was. A pot containing peeled potatoes, which had been on the range ready to be cooked, now lay dashed on the linoleum floor. As the Jacksons stood dumbfounded trying to figure it all out, a plastic bottle of Bold detergent sailed out from the laundry room and plopped to the floor amid the glistening wet potatoes.

"I just don't believe all this!" moaned Etta Jackson. "Are you boys playing some kind of trick on your mother?"

Billy and Mark vigorously denied that they were. Back in the living room once again, they sat down and tried to discuss the strange events rationally.

"None of us was anywhere near those things that fell or went through the air," Billy pointed out.

"We sure weren't," said Mark, backing him up.

"I wonder what's going to happen next?" Mrs. Jackson said apprehensively.

They waited for a couple of minutes, looking at each other with anxious faces. Then they were amazed to see the TV screen light up and hear the voices of the actors as the movie the boys had been watching continued. This seemed to signal the end of the poltergeist activity for that night.

Nothing untoward happened at the Jackson apartment for the next four nights. They even began to make jokes about the ghost. But on the evening of August 17, the disturbances commenced anew . . . and at about the same hour as before.

Mrs. Jackson, home from work, was sitting in her easy chair with her iced tea. The boys were ensconced before the TV set. All of a sudden, Etta Jackson's glass of iced tea began to jiggle and fell with a crash to the floor. Almost at the same moment, a curtain of oscillating "snow" obliterated the picture on the TV, then the set went dead.

"Oh, Lord, it's come back!" wailed Mrs. Jackson.

"What's it going to do next?" wondered Mark aloud.

They had not long to wait. Presently a copy of *Ebony* magazine slid across the coffee table and dropped in a heap on the carpet. A candlestick teetered on the mantelpiece and crashed on the floor below. Then they all witnessed with amazement a box of cookies, which the boys had been eating in the kitchen, sail into the living room and drop at Billy's feet. Next they heard a series of thumps and crashes coming from the bathroom. They found the bathroom cabinet door wide open and into the sink below it had fallen a container of baby powder, two plastic bottles of Vitamin C tablets, a tube of toothpaste, and a bottle of shampoo.

"This is just incredible!" breathed Etta Jackson in a trembling voice. She picked up the articles and put them back in the cabinet. Wandering dazedly back into the living room, they were just in time to see the electric clock on the desk rise into the air, yanking its cord out of the wall, and arc across the room. It slammed into a wall and came to rest on the floor. Feeling suddenly weak and terribly scared, Etta Jackson collapsed into her chair. The boys too sat down, waiting to see if anything else would happen. It soon did. A picture of Billy and Mark on the mantel started rocking precariously, then became airborne for a few feet, and dropped in front of the coffee table. The next event proved to be the most potentially dangerous yet. A heavy serving platter which had been sitting on the kitchen table came flying through the kitchen door, whizzed right at Billy, narrowly missing his head, and smashed to bits on the floor behind him.

"That was a close one!" whispered Billy.

"I'm scared, Ma," whimpered Mark.

After this, nothing happened for about two minutes. Then, as before, the TV screen lit up, apparently signalling the end of the activity for that evening.

Two nights later, about the time Mrs. Jackson got home from work, there was a similar demonstration. She decided to seek some family help. She was worried that there was no man in the house, so she went to see her brother Lester Johnson, who lived close by, and told him the whole story. Lester said that it all sounded like "crazy spook talk," but agreed to come over the next time there was trouble.

This turned out to be on the evening of August 22, when again the TV went dead. Etta quickly phoned Lester, who said he'd be right over. Then, with great trepidation, she and the boys awaited the evening's demonstration. First, they heard a crash coming from the laundry just off the kitchen. They found that a glass bottle of Clorox had toppled off its shelf and smashed on the floor. Lester arrived just in time to see a whole row of books fall one after another, like a line of dominoes, from the book shelf. Next, everyone saw a cut-glass bowl of walnuts on the sideboard elevate into the air, sail across the room diagonally, and smash into a corner, strewing the nuts all over the carpet.

"Do you believe me now, Lester?" asked Etta.

"Now that I've seen it with my own eyes," Lester replied, "I guess I've got to."

"What do you think it is, Uncle Lester?" Billy wanted to know. "Some kind of ghost?"

"Possibly," he said. Lester taught in an elementary school not far from the apartment house. "I once read a book about ghosts, and some of the stories in it sounded just like what's going on here."

Three more events occurred on this evening. In the kitchen, a carton of drain cleaner upended and spattered on the linoleum floor, and the hot water turned on all by itself. In the living room, a framed photograph dropped to the floor, and the glass over it was cracked. Then the TV screen slowly lit up again.

"That means it's over for tonight," Etta told Lester, pointing to the TV. "It always happens like this. Lester, what're we going to do? I'm not so scared for myself, but I am for the boys. Billy almost got hit by that platter the other night."

Lester was shaking his head in bafflement. "Well," he offered, "you could tell the police about it, I suppose."

"No way," said Etta firmly. "Then the whole story could get out. I could lose my job. Folks would think we're crazy or something. No, no cops."

"OK," said Lester, "I guess you'll have to ride it out and wait for the thing to go away. I don't think these things last too long. Look, Sis, try not to worry, OK? Next time—if there is a next time—phone me, and I'll be right over."

Etta did—on the evening of August 25. The TV had gone off, heralding the coming of new disturbances. Lester came over in record time. On this evening, more books fell from the shelf; the refrigerator door was found open and eggs were found smashed in their carton; and a bottle of Windex fell from the laundry shelf and broke on the floor. Then the TV set came on again.

"Well," commented Lester, philosophically, "it wasn't so bad tonight. Maybe it is going to go away soon."

"Lord, I hope so," said Etta. "But I'm still scared for the boys' sake."

On September 3, the poltergeist put in what was to be its

last appearance. It was the most violent of all. After the TV
had gone dead, Lester was summoned, and he came over
immediately. But he missed the first event: the levitation of
the coffee table about six inches off the floor. Then it just
dropped suddenly with a sickening thud, thoroughly frightening Mrs. Jackson and the boys.

"Look out!" yelled Lester, just as he had taken a seat on the
couch. "From the kitchen!"

And through the open kitchen door sailed a heavy skillet,
straight at Billy, who let out a terrified yell. He ducked, and it
just grazed his shoulder before clattering to the floor behind
his chair. Next, the darkened TV began rocking on its table,
but Lester rushed over and steadied it before it fell. Then
there came a series of thunderous knockings on the west
wall of the living room. These lasted a good three minutes by
Lester's watch.

"I'm scared, Ma, *really* scared," whimpered Mark, burying
himself in Mrs. Jackson's arms.

"Maybe that's it for tonight," muttered Lester, looking
around fearfully and still holding on to the TV set.

It wasn't. A minute or so later, the floor lamp by Etta
Jackson's chair tottered and fell, barely missing young Mark.
Next there was a cluster of machinegunlike reports from the
kitchen. Rushing in, Lester and Billy found the door to a
storage cabinet wide open; a dozen or so cans of soup had
been brushed out and onto the floor. As Lester and Billy
were picking them up, the electric quartz clock over the sink
dropped and smashed. At this point, they heard Mrs. Jackson
and Mark yelling to them from the living room, so they
quickly dashed in there.

"Look, Uncle Lester," shouted Mark in a shaky voice. "The
TV! It's going back on!" And so it was.

"That must be the end of it for this time," said Lester.

". . . until *next* time," Billy put in.

"That does it!" declared Etta Jackson decisively. "For you kids there's not going to be any next time. Tomorrow morning we're going to send you off for a visit to Aunt Nettie's. I don't care if school's starting or not."

As good as her word, Mrs. Jackson got Billy and Mark packed up next day and sent them off to her sister Nettie, who lived not far away in Gary, Indiana. With their departure—or at least in their absence—no more disturbances occurred in the apartment. Neither did anything strange happen at Aunt Nettie's. After the boys had been gone for three weeks, Etta consulted with Lester about the wisdom of bringing them home again, for they had already missed several days of school.

"Give it a try," advised Lester. "After all, they can't stay at Nettie's forever. It may be that this thing's run its course by now."

Evidently it had, for when the boys came back again, there proved to be no more disturbances. When it was switched on, the TV stayed on and didn't go dead. And all the items in the apartment remained in their proper places.

So it was that this case of poltergeist activity finally came to light. In all probability, the occurrences were centering around the "focus person" of teen-aged Billy Jackson. In some way, the adolescent may have been subconsciously troubled—so much so that his tensions inadvertently released powerful psychic forces that resulted in the disturbances. Indeed, he may even have been directing these forces at his own person, for it was he who was nearly hit with the heavy platter and skillet. In any event, the case was a remarkable one on two counts: the regularity of the poltergeist's arrival at a few minutes past 6 P.M. on each occasion and its habit of announcing its comings and goings via the TV set.

THE
HAUNTED
CHURCH
IN
ESSEX

THIS CASE IS SIGNIFICANT IN THE LITERATURE OF PSYCHIC research because it involved the rare combination of apparitions, poltergeist disturbances, and tactile phenomena. It occurred in the old church—torn down due to decay in the 1960s—which stood near the manor house at Langenhoe near Colchester in Essex. Indeed, the church has been called the most haunted one in England, and it once looked out over bleak marshes adjacent to the Strait of Dover.

The principal figure in the case was the Reverend E. A. Merryweather, a clergyman of sound judgment and much humor, who before becoming rector at Langenhoe in 1937 had lived most of his life in the north of England. He had had no experience in occult matters, nor did the subject interest him in the least. But when the strange occurrences began the year he arrived at the Langenhoe rectory, he started noting them down in a journal.

The odd disturbances, which suggested to Reverend Merryweather that something was amiss about the place, consisted largely of poltergeist events of a fairly common nature. "I visited the church on September 20, 1937," he wrote in his journal. "It was a quiet autumn day. I was standing alone in the church, and the big west door was open. Suddenly it crashed to with such force that the whole building seemed to shake. Doors don't slam to as if an express-train had hit them when there is no palpable reason. This aroused my curiosity as to the cause."

The following month, the clergyman experienced another strange event—not once but twice. He had a small traveling bag in which he carried books and his vestments, and it had a lock on it. Twice he found it unaccountably locked while in the vestry. On both occasions, try as he would, he could not get the bag unlocked while he was in the church or near it. Only when he got out onto the road leading to the church would the lock become unfastened. The first time it happened a friend was with the rector and observed this strange occurrence.

After that, and all during the years of World War II, little happened that was worth noting down in his journal. But as the war ended in 1945, the first of several incidents involving flowers in the church took place. A member of the congregation and her daughter were helping Merryweather decorate the church with flowers. They had put some flowers in a vase on a certain pew, then had gone away to do something else. A few moments later the woman returned to find the flowers taken out of the vase and lying beside it on the pew. Subsequently, there were other occasions when flowers simply appeared out of nowhere or just disappeared.

Two years later in the fall of 1947, Reverend Merryweather experienced the first of the tactile phenomena. He paid a visit to the manor house nearby, which was then occupied by a Mrs. Cutting. She asked the rector if he would like to see the house, and Merryweather said he would. When they entered one of the front bedrooms, Mrs. Cutting remarked that she never used the room, for there appeared to be something strange about it. She then left the room, saying, "I don't like this room."

Now alone in the room, the rector went to the window and stood admiring the view for a minute or so. When he finally turned to leave, he later said, "I moved into the unmistakable embrace of a young woman." This tactile experience lasted for only a few seconds, but there was no doubt about it in his mind whatsoever. As the rector put it, "One wild, frantic embrace and she was gone." Furthermore, Merryweather reported that nothing else accompanied the touching sensation. He had seen nothing, heard nothing, and smelled nothing.

The next year, 1948, as he was celebrating Holy Communion, the rector and everyone in the congregation heard loud thumping noises coming from the direction of the vestry. This occurred on several occasions, and each time Merryweather conducted an investigation; but nothing was ever found. Through the summer they continued with regularity, but then tapered off through the winter months. In November, the rector happened to be raking a pile of coal at the side of the church with an iron staff. As he was doing so, he suddenly sensed that something or someone was standing close to him. Deciding to perform a test, he jammed the iron staff down into the coal pile, removed his square cleric's cap, and put it on the end of the staff. He was astounded to see the cap start to slowly rotate before his eyes—all by itself.

A few minutes after this incident, the rector said that he

heard what sounded like voices coming from the empty church. Fearing that some local vandals might be causing the commotion, Merryweather decided to go armed into his house of worship. He had a knife that his son in the Middle East had sent him, and he stuck this in his belt underneath his cassock and, with some trepidation, entered the church. As he was standing in front of the altar, he felt the knife being snatched from his belt by some unseen force. He both saw and heard it clatter to the stone floor by his feet. Simultaneously, he heard the voice of a woman hiss, "You are a cruel man." Thinking it over later, Merryweather believed that the voice came from the part of the church which housed the building's tower. So ended the weird events of that November day, and the rector noted them down in his journal.

Early in December, Merryweather and some of his congregation heard more inexplicable noises in the church. They appeared to emanate from a sealed-off entryway, originally a private entrance to the church for occupants of the manor house. To those who heard them, the sounds resembled someone coughing. A few seconds later, a small bell on the table bearing the sacraments of Holy Communion started to ring—with no one at all near it. This was shortly followed by what sounded to everyone like the report of a rifle shot. A search was made but nothing amiss was discovered. For the next several months, lamps were seen to swing of their own accord in the church, and often the small bell was heard to ring with no one near it.

It was on August 21, 1949, that Reverend Merryweather first saw the apparition of a young woman in the church. That day he was celebrating Communion. As he turned to read from the Bible at the altar, he looked down the aisle and saw a woman of about thirty walking from the tower side of

the church across toward where the choir normally sat. The rector noted that she was wearing a grayish dress with some kind of "flowing headgear" that hung over her shoulders. When she reached the southwest corner of the church, she seemed to pass right through the stone wall and vanish. Oddly, she made no sound, appeared to stoop a bit as she walked, and looked absolutely solid rather than transparent.

For the rest of the year there occurred other strange events. These included mysterious knockings and footsteps inside the church, the smashing of a vestry door-handle, and the inexplicable locking of this same door. One night in September a friend of the rector's, a distinguished psychical researcher, stayed overnight at Langenhoe and set up some elaborate equipment about the church and even the churchyard. Doors and windows were sealed, powdered chalk was strewn about where the apparition had been seen, string was strung at key points, and other measures were taken to detect any ghostly activity. However, a terrible storm raged all that night and the noise of thunder and the rain may have blocked out any auditory phenomena that may have occurred. In any case, in the morning when the research equipment was checked, nothing had been disturbed.

During the fall of 1950, a new phenomenon was added to the already impressive array of paranormal happenings at the church. When the rector entered his sanctuary on September 14, he smelled a peculiar odor suffusing the whole place. It was, said Merryweather, that of violets—then, of course, completely out of season. A few days later, while Merryweather was in the vestry, he could clearly hear the voice of a young woman singing somewhere in the west portion of the church. Later he described the singing as sounding like a Gregorian chant. Then the singing stopped, and Merryweather heard heavy noises resembling a man's footsteps; they were, he said, apparently walking up the nave "with slow and sinister tread." Leaving the vestry to investigate, he entered the church proper but could find nothing to account for the singing or the footfalls. A week to the day after this incident, as the rector stepped into the churchyard bound for the vestry, he spied two workmen at the church door trying to look through the keyhole. They beckoned to him to join them, which Merryweather did. They said they had heard some singing coming from within and wondered who the singers might be. The church at that hour was locked and supposedly empty. Then Merryweather himself could hear the singing—which seemed to be in French! Abruptly the singing stopped, and the rector unlocked the heavy door and entered with the two men. The three searched everywhere but could find no one at all in the church.

On Christmas Eve that same year, Reverend Merryweather saw another apparition in his sanctuary. This time it was not the phantom of a woman, but of a man. Coming into the church late in the afternoon, he saw a figure gliding along up the nave toward the chancel. It appeared to have materialized from out of nowhere, and the rector stopped short and watched it. It looked to him like a man wearing a tweed suit. As he gaped at it, the form seemed to merge with the pulpit and then vanished.

Near the end of January of the new year, Reverend Merryweather arrived at the church and went into the vestry to do some work. But as he did so, he noticed some dead flowers in his office, so he took them into the churchyard and threw them away. As he returned, he noticed there was a white impression of a woman's hand on his vestry door. It was a clear imprint, as if it had been made with some kind of powder; but no powder was present. This curious effect remained for nearly two weeks, then gradually faded away. The rector's housekeeper and her daughter also saw the imprint.

The next major event happened that summer. Early in July Reverend Merryweather again saw the apparition of the woman with the flowing headgear. She was dressed exactly as she had been the first time he saw her. On this occasion she was standing near the altar, facing the sacraments table with the small bell on it and the old entryway—now bricked up—once used by the manor house family. As Merryweather watched, she began to float toward the bricked-up door and just vanished into it. About a month after this episode, the rector arrived at the church one morning and was puzzled to hear voices. It sounded to him as if two or three persons were talking in low voices near the chancel. He could not make out any of the words, but at length he heard one of the voices sigh ponderously. Then the talking ceased. Going into the sanctuary, he looked all about but no one was there.

During the spring and summer of 1952, other events occurred of a paranormal nature. The lid of the organ was seen to move by itself; loud bangs and door rattlings were heard, as well as popping noises and footsteps; and once an unlit candle suddenly burst into flame and then went out. It was in mid-October of that year that Reverend Merryweather glimpsed yet another apparition in his church. As he stood at the altar reading a Psalm, he felt an eerie sensation that somebody was watching him. Turning, he saw the figure of a young woman—not the same one as twice before—who was staring at him from some distance away. She was wearing a cream-colored dress, and she had an oval face with blue eyes. The rector said she gave him a "strange, sad look" and then disappeared; he also claimed that her dress seemed to linger for a few seconds after the wearer had vanished.

During his tenure at Langenhoe, Reverend Merryweather learned some local stories that might possibly account for the hauntings. The most likely of them involved a former rector who was said to have murdered his secret sweetheart. Conceivably, the earthbound spirit of the wronged girl—the apparition he saw twice—would have chosen another rector—Merryweather—to appear to. A knife was supposedly the weapon used, and perhaps this may have accounted for some force knocking the knife out of Merryweather's cassock on one occasion. The whispered conversation on another occasion might possibly be linked to the whispering of lovers, and the final sigh heard that of the girl's last breathing—somehow preserved in the psychic atmosphere. The tweedy figure may have been the materialized apparition of the guilty rector's earthbound spirit, haunting the scene of his crime. The young woman felt by Merryweather in the manor house bedroom may have been a tactile apparition of the murdered girl. Other parallels and connections could also be made, as Reverend Merryweather well knew, but they were also speculations which could never be proved. In any event, he retired in 1959, and the Langenhoe rectorship was combined with that of a nearby parish. Not long afterward, the decaying and haunted church, together with its ghosts, was torn down.

Yet the case remains an important one in the annals of the occult. Few others have incorporated practically the whole gamut of unexplained ghostly manifestations—apparitions, poltergeist occurrences galore, touching sequences, and even the out-of-season smell of violets.

THE GHOST OF DAVID McCONNEL

ONE OF THE BEST-DOCUMENTED CASES CONCERNING A MAN who witnessed the dying apparition of his wartime friend occurred in England during World War I. The case was first recorded in Mrs. Henry Sidgwick's updated version of Edmund Gurney's classic pioneer work in psychical research *Phantasms of the Living*. Mrs. Sidgwick's edition appeared in 1923, five years after the event occurred. The case was also recorded in the *Proceedings* of the British Society for Psychical Research and was well vouched for in all details by several competent witnesses of the Royal Flying Corps, later to be redesignated the Royal Air Force (RAF). The *Proceedings* article was authored by another pioneer researcher W. H. Salter, a meticulous investigator in occult matters.

The facts of the case were these: On December 7, 1918, at

3:25 P.M., Lieutenant David McConnel, while flying his Sopwith Camel from Scampton, Lincolnshire, to Tadcaster Airdrome, was killed when his plane crashed during the flight. The accident was witnessed, and McConnel's wrist-watch, which had stopped at 3:25 P.M., fixed the exact time of the tragedy. At the young flier's funeral on December 11, his father learned that one of his son's friends, a Lieutenant Larkin, had had a vision of him at about the same time as the crash. Mr. McConnel then wrote a letter to Larkin, asking him to describe his experience in detail. Larkin wrote back immediately to the grieving father.

David, reported Lieutenant Larkin, had been dressed in his flying clothes around 11:00 A.M. of the fatal day. He went to the hangars where he intended to take a plane to the Aerial Range for some machine-gun practice. Larkin thought nothing of this, for it was a routine occurrence for all pilots. At this time he was in the pilots' quarters which he shared with McConnel.

Larkin was surprised, however, when he saw David walk back into their room just a half hour later. David then announced that he was not going to the Aerial Range after all. He had been ordered by the commanding officer to fly a Camel over to Tadcaster Airdrome, where it was needed for training purposes.

"I expect to be back in time for tea," he had told Lieutenant Larkin. "Cheerio!"

David then walked out of the room, said Larkin, but a minute or so later he saw McConnel rapping on the window from outside. David asked him to hand him his map, which he had forgotten, and Larkin did so. Soon after this, Larkin said that he had gone to noon mess, then had spent most of the early afternoon sitting in front of the stove fire writing letters and reading.

Larkin wrote that he had been sitting like this in front of the fire, the door of the room being about eight feet behind him, when he heard someone walking up the hall. He then heard the door burst open with David's usual noise and clatter.

Larkin said that he had turned half-way around in his chair and had seen David McConnel standing in the door-way, half in and half out of the room, holding the door knob in his hand. He was dressed in his full flying clothes, but wearing his naval cap, and there was nothing unusual in his appearance. (Later, investigators considered the mention of the naval cap as being an important corroborative detail in

the case. Earlier, David had been in the Royal Navy's flying service and was very proud of this. When he later transferred to the Royal Flying Corps, he always wore the naval flying uniform about the airdrome or, if he had to wear the RFC flying equipment, he still insisted on wearing his naval cap as a reminder of his connection with that service.) Larkin, in his long letter to David's father, reported that he had seen the naval cap pushed jauntily back on David's head—exactly the way he always wore it. He also wrote that David was smiling, as he always did when he entered the room.

"Hello, boy," Larkin heard him say clearly.

"Hello," Larkin replied. "Back already?"

"Yes," David answered. "Got there all right, had a good trip."

Larkin wrote Mr. McConnel that he couldn't be positively sure of the exact words David had used. But he had said, "Had a good trip," or "Had a fine trip," or words to that effect. Larkin added that he had been looking at his friend the whole time he'd been speaking. David's final words had been these: "Well, cheerio!"

Larkin had then watched David close the door in his noisy fashion and go out. Larkin wrote that he had gone on with his reading, thinking that probably David had gone to visit some friends in the other rooms, or perhaps had gone back to the hangar for some of his flying gear, or for something else that he had forgotten.

At the time, Larkin reported that he had not had a watch, but he was certain it was between a quarter and half-past three. Larkin said he was certain of this because shortly afterward another pilot, Lieutenant Garner-Smith, had entered the room and told him the time was a quarter to four. Garner-Smith had then remarked to Larkin: "I hope Mac (David) gets back early. We're going to Lincoln this evening."

"He *is* back," Larkin had replied. "He was in the room just a few minutes ago."

"Is he having tea?" Garner-Smith wanted to know.

Larkin had answered that he didn't think so because David had not changed out of his flying clothes, and he was probably in one of the other rooms chatting with friends.

"Well," Garner-Smith then said, "I'll try and find him."

After this interchange, Larkin wrote that he had gone and had his own tea, after which he returned to his quarters, dressed, and went to Lincoln for the evening.

While Larkin was in the smoking room of the Albion Hotel that night, he said that he had heard a group of officers talking and overheard in their conversation the words "crashed," "Tadcaster," and "McConnel." Larkin said that he joined them, and they proceeded to tell him that just before they had left Scampton, word had come through that McConnel had crashed and been killed taking his Camel to Tadcaster.

At that moment, Larkin reported, he had not believed the story, because his impression was that David had gone up again after he had last seen him—for he was positive he had seen him at about 3:30 in the afternoon. Naturally eager to hear something more definite about the matter, Larkin did some more inquiring and learned that David, in fact, had been killed on the Tadcaster flight.

Next morning, Larkin said that he had a long discussion with Garner-Smith about his strange experience. Garner-Smith tried to persuade him that he must have been mistaken, that he had not actually seen David on the previous afternoon about 3:30. But Larkin continued to insist that he *had* seen him.

Larkin finished his letter to David's father with these words: "As you can understand, Mr. McConnel, I was at a loss to solve the problem. There was no disputing the fact that he *had* been killed whilst flying to Tadcaster, as we ascertained afterwards that his watch had stopped at 3:25. I tried to persuade myself that I had not seen him or spoken to him in this room, but could not make myself believe otherwise, as I was undeniably awake and his appearance, voice, manner had all been so natural. I am of such a skeptical nature regarding things of this kind that even now I wish to think otherwise, that I did not see him, but I am unable to do so."

Lieutenant Larkin had no doubt as to the identity of the man he saw, and later he wrote that the room he had been sitting in was a small one; the electric heater was on and also a good fire was burning in an open stove. "I may mention," he added, "that the light was particularly good and bright, and there were no shadows or half-shadows in the room."

Viewing this as a dying apparition case, W. H. Salter presented the theory that David McConnel, fatigued by the long flight, may not have known that he was crashing. Instead, he may have imagined that he had already arrived safely at Tadcaster, had taken off again, and was back at Scampton. But this hypothesis hardly holds water. Rather, it seems more likely that the spirit of the newly-dead man felt somehow impelled to carry out his usual routine after a flight—one that he still believed he had successfully completed—of reporting back to his quarters, seeing his friends, and then having tea.

THE MILLVILLE, IOWA, POLTERGEIST

NOT ONLY WAS THIS POLTERGEIST CASE UNUSUAL IN several respects, but it attracted nationwide attention toward the end of 1959 and the beginning of 1960. Wire services picked up reports of it; radio and television stations gave it a big play; and *Newsweek* magazine deemed it important enough to list in its compilation of weekly news items.

The disturbances occurred in an Iowa farmhouse in the valley country in Millville, not far from the larger town of Guttenberg on the Mississippi River. "The ghost house," penned one inspired newspaper writer, was situated "at the dead end of a branch off Split Level Road where black crows abound in the creek valley and outcroppings of rocks jut forth like vultures."

The headline-provoking occurrences began on Thanksgiving night, 1959, in the home of William Meyer. Normally a spry 83-year-old man, Meyer at this time was in bed convalescing from a broken hip. So that he could enjoy the company of his family, Meyer had his bed moved down into a corner of the living room. Meyer's wife was comfortably settled in an easy chair across the room and his grandson Gene was sitting on the edge of his bed. As was often the family custom in the evening, the lights were turned off as they rested.

All of a sudden, a very loud noise was heard above them which startled them and threw them into, as Meyer's wife later said, "a tizzy." When Mrs. Meyer switched the lights back on, she and her husband were astonished to see that Gene's face was coated with a blackish, sooty kind of substance. Moreover, the odious, dusty stuff had settled in a clinging layer all over the living room. William Meyer then told Gene to go summon his father, Elmer, who resided on the adjoining farm. When Elmer arrived, he found his mother in the act of trying to clean up the mess with some dustpans. Elmer commented later that the substance was "wet and gray like soot."

The whole Meyer family couldn't figure out what the sooty material was or where it had come from. Their faithful woodburning stove had not been injured in any way, nor were there any holes or cracks in its pipes. The windows had been closed during the incident, and the walls and ceilings were as solid as ever. For the next several days, William's wife talked about the mysterious "real fine dirt" that had been deposited that night, and Gene was kidded a lot about the "black face" it had given him. All freely discussed the event with neighbors, trying to figure out what had caused it.

Christmas was approaching, however, and the event was almost forgotten—until the evening of December 16. On this occasion, Gene was once again sitting in the living room with his grandparents. As usual at this hour, the lights had been switched off for a while. Suddenly the Meyers heard a terrifically loud thud. When Gene hit the light switch, they found that a wooden flower stand had fallen over and a bowl filled with some Christmas cards atop it had skittered across the room and come to rest under William Meyer's bed. As the family nervously argued over this latest event, Mrs. Meyer saw a glass of water elevate from a nearby table, rise over her head, and spill all over her.

As before, Gene was dispatched to call Elmer, his father, to come to the home. After inspecting this disturbance Elmer, a down-to-earth farmer, came up with a theory. Some kind of natural vibrations, he propounded, had to be causing these strange occurrences. He decided to test his theory by placing an egg on top of a lamp shade and instructing everyone to watch closely to see if it moved. Before he left for his own home, Elmer watched for two hours, but the egg remained in its precarious position.

When Elmer had gone, Gene remarked, "Everything else has happened in the dark. Maybe if we turn out the lights, things will start happening again." This sounded like a good idea, so Gene turned off the lights. Once again the three Meyers sat in the dark—this time waiting to see if Elmer's "vibrations" from some natural source would move the egg. After about two minutes had gone by, they heard a number of loud, mushy-sounding *splats*. When the lights were switched back on, everyone saw that the egg was smashed against the door and several clumps of mud were found sticking on the wall.

Shocked as they were by these events, the Meyers decided

not to call Elmer over again that night. Gene and his grand-
mother cleaned up the mess as best they could. Then Gene
left for home to tell his father of these latest developments.

The following day the poltergeist activity became so intense that it frightened the elder Meyers. As dusk was
coming on, they heard loud noises overhead. William Meyer
commented later that they sounded like "nine or ten men
upstairs knocking boards off the roof." These continued for
nearly half an hour. Just as Mrs. Meyer bravely started
supper, they heard some loud crashes in the milk pantry. She
discovered that an old refrigerator, used to store jars and
bottles, had been tipped over on the floor. In its fall it had
knocked down some milk-separating equipment and a table

loaded with dishes. It was the first time during the occurrences that teen-aged Gene Meyer had not been on the scene. He had gone on an errand, and later his father confirmed the fact that he had seen him outside his grandparents' house during the dramatic events in the milk pantry.

At any rate, the elderly couple, having had enough of "this spook business," moved out of the house temporarily and went to live with relatives in Guttenberg. Later William Meyer told two psychic investigators, "I didn't know what would have happened next; if I'd stayed, I would probably be dead now." Subsequently, one of the relatives in Guttenberg commented, "We don't want them to go back until we know what's happening down there. The whole house might be swallowed up—that's limestone country, you know, and there's springs—water might have opened up a hole under the house." And Elmer Meyer, still sticking to his vibrational theory, pointed out, "There's a spring on one side of the house, and a creek runs by the other. That might cause some of these things somehow."

A couple of days after his parents had vacated the house, Elmer showed a local photographer about the premises. As they went down into the basement, a huge rock dislodged itself from one of the walls and smashed a ten-gallon crock. Later, on New Year's Day, 1960, Elmer asked Clayton County Sheriff Forrest Fischer to accompany him on a thorough investigation of the farmhouse. Fischer agreed to go, but declared that he thought the whole business was "a bunch of hokus-pokus." On that day, Elmer, Fischer, and three local reporters walked through the house. As they did so, one of the newsmen saw a bottle fly out of a packing case and smash itself on the cement floor. The reporters began to accuse each other of pulling a prank, but all denied having done the deed.

On January 6, a Wednesday, some of Elmer Meyer's friends said they intended to spend the night in the haunted house. Among them was a giant of a man named Pat Livingston. Pat weighed over 260 pounds and was a much-respected river-boat pilot on the Mississippi. That night the husky pilot became personally involved with the poltergeist when he was unceremoniously thrown out of bed. Later he told reporters, "Look, I'm no crackpot. I don't believe it, but it happened, all right."

Pat had gone to bed that night earlier than his companions, who were still sitting in the kitchen talking. A little past 10 P.M., while he was still awake, the burly pilot saw the chair beside his bed begin to glide away from him. "The thing bobbled across the floor for about eight feet and tipped over," he later reported. "I thought maybe some of the other people had tied a string on it and pulled it away, but they all denied it."

Just as Livingston was settling back down in his bed to sleep, it suddenly happened: " . . .the next thing I knew, I was lying on the floor. I'll take a lie detector test or anything. I woke up kind of groggy. I wouldn't have believed it for love or money." Furthermore, the big pilot declared, nothing human had shoved him off the bed that night. "None of the people present were big enough to do it," he explained. "And when anyone grabs me, I grab back!"

In the farmhouse that night was young Gene Meyer. He later said, "Pat was going to make a big joke out of the whole haunting business. But he was the most surprised man I've ever seen."

By now the publicity concerning the disturbances at Millville was in full swing. Scientists, professors, and students from nearby colleges interested in such matters, as well as curiosity seekers, began descending on the once lonely little farmhouse. Some of the university people brought elaborate equipment. Oscilloscopes, ion counters, argon radiation machines, and Geiger counters were set up in the vacated house. Teams of professors and students kept a 24-hour vigil night after night, as they tried to ensnare the poltergeist with their electronic gadgetry.

Their results, however, were less than startling. The argon radiation device, for instance, discovered no fault or crack in the surrounding bedrock. The oscilloscope registered only the normal 60-cycle sine-wave "picked up from the house wiring." The Geiger counter indicated nothing save "normal residual radiation." The ion counter, declared a physics professor, "registered a high negative reading when we first came into the room, which is unusual, but after the air had circulated a little, the readings were quite normal." And a group of University of Iowa students reported no strange noise during the night, except for "a guy snoring downstairs."

When the two psychical researchers finally arrived, one from California and the other from New York, the only active disturbances were being caused, not by a poltergeist, but by the rowdy crowd that gathered each night outside the farmhouse. Indeed, the whole case now rapidly deteriorated into a ugly mob scene. One staff writer for a Dubuque newspaper wrote of the worst night of all inside the ghost house when the "insiders" practically had to do battle with the "outsiders." When Elmer Meyer denied the "outsiders" entrance to the house, the mob started to pound furiously on the door, until it seemed it would soon break down.

Just at this moment, the "insiders" threw open the door and fired off photographers' flashbulbs, temporarily blinding the leaders of the mob. Another band of "outsiders" forced their way into the cellar and started to pour up into the house. These too were driven off by a battery of flash-bulbs. At length, reports that the sheriff was on his way to the scene sent the hooligan element roaring away in their cars.

After the two researchers held extensive interviews with the witnesses in the case, they came to the conclusion that many of the disturbances could conceivably be attributed to misinterpretation of natural mishaps and psychological expectancy on the part of human agents. However, they could not rule out the possibility that psychic forces may also have been responsible for the strange events.

Other investigators commented that the case seemed to center about the teen-ager, Gene Meyer. Except for the events in the milk pantry, he was present during all the poltergeist disturbances. And even on that day, he was in the immediate vicinity. As so often in poltergeist cases, this young man may have been subconsciously upset about something—so much so that powerful psychic forces may have been unleashed to cause the poltergeist manifestations.

TWO WOMEN AND THE GHOSTS OF DIEPPE

FROM THE BALCONY OF A SMALL FRENCH HOTEL IN PUYS during the early morning hours of August 4, 1951, two women peered out toward the restless waters of the English Channel. Their hotel was only a mile east of Dieppe, site of the famous—and disastrous—Allied raid in 1942 on targets in occupied France during World War II. The women stood stock-still, incredulous and frightened. Although the surrounding countryside was perfectly tranquil, they were listening to sounds which, minute for minute, matched those of the bitter battle that had raged nine years before. At the time, they did not realize they were audibly witnessing—hearing—the sounds of the famous raid. They merely continued to listen in fearful fascination.

The women could hear the raucous noise of battle rolling

74

and reverberating all around them. Through the pre-dawn summer haze came the rumble of naval gunfire, the whine of dive bombers, and the frantic shouting of commands. Their ears also picked up clearly the *whump* of mortar shells exploding, the snapping of rifle fire, and the deadly chatter of machine guns. More moving still to the women were the pitiful cries of wounded and dying men. There was no mistaking that they were hearing the horrible cacophony of war. Later they would learn that they were listening to the assault of ten thousand Allied troops tumbling ashore from landing craft and fighting desperately on the beaches of Dieppe.

This eerie scene was audibly witnessed by two English-women on a holiday with their children in France. One, Dorothy, was the wife of a Member of Parliament and the other was her sister-in-law, Agnes. The previous day had been a hot one, and they had spent it on the beach. Then they had returned to the hotel, eaten with their children, and put them to bed. Feeling tired about 11 P.M., the two went upstairs to their second-floor room, with a balcony that faced the sea.

Shortly after 4 A.M., Agnes awoke, having heard an uncanny sound. At first she thought it was far-off thunder heralding an approaching storm. As the seconds ticked away, it grew louder and more insistent. Agnes went on listening, and the heightening noise now seemed to be coming from the beach. Straining to hear more clearly, she thought she heard men yelling and the strident growl of distant thunder.

At this point, Dorothy awoke. "What's that noise?" she asked.

Agnes shook her head in complete puzzlement. "I can't imagine," she answered in a whisper. "I've been listening to it for three or four minutes."

Dorothy, however, had served in the armed forces during the recent war, and there was little doubt in her mind what the noise was; it was the sound of battle. Later, she wrote in her own account of the experience, "It sounded like a roar which ebbed and flowed. We could distinctly hear the sounds of cries, shouts, and gunfire."

The two women got out of bed and went cautiously out on

the small balcony. Nothing at all was moving. There was not even a car on the road leading to the beach, nor was there a soul astir on the sleepy main street of Puys. While they could see no troops in the direction of the beach, they could hear men shouting commands and others moaning piteously. In addition, they could hear the crackle of star shells exploding, but they could not see their lights. Yet all too real was the screech of shells passing overhead and the crescendo of desperate cries coming from the beach.

The watching women were both surprised when, at 4:50 A.M., all sounds abruptly stopped. A quarter of an hour later, however, the whole scenario began anew—this time very quickly reaching a fresh pitch of intensity. The drone of aircraft was especially recognizable. Fighters and dive bombers whined over the dunes, and the aerial bombardment grew louder. Presently, Dorothy and Agnes could detect the rumble of tanks rattling by the hotel itself—but no scoring of track marks could be seen by the women on the nearby sandy road.

Again, at 5:40 A.M., there came another lull in the battle. But ten minutes later, the echoes of pitched warfare recommenced, with the roar of aircraft becoming the most pronounced. Until shortly before 7:00 A.M. the raging noise of battle continued at varying levels of intensity. Mortar shells whumped, naval rounds blasted the ground, machine guns ripped the air and pocked into the beach sands, men yelled and groaned.

Then, around 7 o'clock, the two jittery and fascinated women heard what appeared to be the final shots being fired. The sounds of heavy tank treads and whining aircraft engines receded in the direction of the beach. A peaceful silence again descended on Puys and the hotel. Birds began to sing in the moist morning air. A gentle sea breeze came up, blowing inland steadily, cooling the perspiring women. Agnes and Dorothy looked at each other with red-rimmed, mystified eyes. What on earth, each wondered, had they just witnessed with their ears?

Later that day, Dorothy and Agnes questioned other guests staying at the hotel. Had they been disturbed by the tumult in the early morning hours? Not a single one had. Their children, too, had slept soundly all night and had heard nothing. Why, wondered the thoroughly perplexed women, had no one else heard the infernal din that had been so audible to them?

Luckily, Agnes and Dorothy had made fairly detailed notes concerning the lulls and intensifications of the battle as it progressed. Using these notes, each woman wrote a separate account of what they had heard and sent them to the British Society for Psychical Research in London. By this time the women had made the connection in their minds between what they had heard and the famous Dieppe raid of nine years before. They had reached the conclusion that in some inexplicable way, through some weird trick of time, they had been able to tune in on the sounds of the battle which had occurred in August. This conclusion they also passed on to the British Society.

Investigators at the Society were intrigued by their experience. Consulting a number of military men, they followed up on the accounts written by the two women. Soon they worked out a timetable of events as they occurred during the raid, then they checked them against the accounts of the women. Incredibly, it was found that the times of the attacks, lulls, and periods of naval gunfire and aircraft activity tallied exactly.

However, wondered the researchers, might not Agnes and Dorothy have read up somewhere on the times of the

various attacks and other movements in some official account and then incorporated them into their own accounts?
The answer was no, because the official account of the
Dieppe raid was not published by the military until five
months *after* the women's experience!

The researchers also considered the possibility that the
sounds had come from a nearby movie theater in the area
showing documentary war footage. But there was no cin-
ema in Puys, nor had there been any radio programs of such
a nature broadcast at that time. Could the terrible din of
battle the women had heard have been army maneuvers,
artillery practice, or some similar military activity? These
theories were also ruled out, for no one else at the hotel or
indeed in the whole area had heard any such sounds of
warfare.

Both women were subsequently interviewed individually
by several investigators. One reported, "They struck me as
sane, well-balanced women with no tendency to add color to
their accounts. I think the experience must be rated as a
genuine psychic phenomenon. After all, what other explanation is there?" Other investigators all agreed on one thing:
the women were of undoubted integrity. And it was noted
that in every instance they shunned publicity rather than
sought it.

Had these two women, through some artifice of time,
tuned in to the sounds of a battle fought nine years before?
Did they somehow, for a few hours, enter into a new dimension where long-dead sounds are preserved? Or had the
spirits of the dead who had fallen at Dieppe rerun a scenario
in sound especially for Dorothy and Agnes?

Actually, the case is a classic one of *retrocognition*, one in
which knowledge of past events is obtained by supernatural
means. The odd aspect of the case, however, was that it was

a purely auditory one—nothing was actually seen. One writer on occult matters has put forth the theory that the two women were obviously highly psychic individuals. Then the writer asked this apt question: "Is it too much like a plot of television's *Twilight Zone* to suppose that scenes from wars have imprinted themselves on the psychic ether, to reappear to certain psychic individuals afterwards?"

THE
GHOSTS
OF
HOWLEY HALL
LINKS

WELL OVER 100 MILES NORTHWEST OF LONDON IN YORK-shire there are two industrial towns, Batley and Morley. Between them, on an east-west axis, stretches a broad bluff upon which lies the grassy acreage of Howley Hall Golf Club. The links seem a peaceful spot. The dying sun on a summer's evening dapples and softens the harshly chiseled outlines of the chimneys and roofs of the working towns below. Howley Hall itself, once a splendid stone manor house, now lies in ruins, its tumbled walls overgrown with brush and tangled vines. What was once its sturdy foundation is now but a heap of stones cascading down a bleak knoll. The old farmhouse adjoining the ruins, however, is still intact and serves as headquarters of the club, as well as a tranquil retreat for its members.

Yet the Howley Hall Golf Club is not as peaceful as it looks. Many eyewitnesses claim it is haunted by not one ghost but several. Queer, aimless apparitions are seen to wander over the fairways and putting green, then simply fade away. Often these phantoms seem to be dressed in seventeenth-century attire, for the golf course is situated on land rich in violent associations with the period of the English Civil War.

Once in the late 1960s, a local mathematics teacher and his wife were strolling along the edge of the links at twilight. Just as they reached the ruins of the old Hall, the wife abruptly stopped and stared. She called her husband's attention to a strange figure about forty yards from where they were standing.

"Who do you suppose that woman is?" she asked. "Look at her dress. Isn't it strange?"

Her husband, who now could see the figure too, nodded in agreement.

The wife recalled later, "She was wearing a sort of 'maxi' dress with a dark top. And she had a curious red-colored mantilla veil over her face and shoulders. I remarked to my husband about her, and he agreed with me that there was something rather odd about her appearance when, suddenly, she faded away and vanished right before our eyes. There's very little cover in the area and, in any case, we both saw her. We couldn't understand where she went to. We searched around the whole place, but there was no trace of her."

The schoolteacher, not a man who believed in ghosts of any sort, added, "I find it hard to believe that the lady my wife and I saw was a ghost. And yet she seems to fit the storybook formula for ghostly behavior. We both saw her and we both watched her vanish, but we don't have any rational explanation of it."

Not long after this couple's experience, a local mill worker chanced to be walking along the golf links at just about the same spot. The time of day was also about the same—early evening. Suddenly he too saw a strange-looking woman. Then he noticed that two men were with her.

"At first," explained the mill worker later, "I thought they were golfers. They were standing in a group looking toward Batley and wearing rather dark loose-fitting clothes. My dog ran toward them and I called him back. As I did so, they simply vanished. I didn't exactly see them go—but there was nowhere else they could have gone to. The spot where they stood and the hillside below it was totally deserted."

A much different experience—but no less real to the person it happened to—was reported by one of the Howley Hall club members. A very practical and respected man, he was a director of one of the local mills.

"I was going around the course on my own," he related, "and I think there was one other twosome, well ahead of me. I was feeling very relaxed and was looking forward to a couple of drinks at the clubhouse when I suddenly had the most peculiar feeling. Dusk was drawing on, and I was just about to make a short putt when I felt certain I was being watched. I paused and looked around, but there was nobody in my vicinity at all. It was as if a whole crowd of invisible watchers were standing around the green, surrounding me. The experience was most stifling and unpleasant. I felt terribly depressed all of a sudden and couldn't get away from there quickly enough."

If phantoms wander aimlessly across the fairways of Howley Hall golf links, there is probably good reason for them to do so. For the whole history of the area abounds with stories of bloodshed and violent death.

The nobleman who built Howley Hall was an able but melancholy man named Sir John Savile. Upon his death

there in 1630, his son, Viscount Thomas Savile, inherited the estate. With the outbreak of the English Civil War, he went off to fight on the side of the king, leaving the Hall and grounds in the hands of a relative, Sir John Savile of Lupset. In June 1643 the royalist Duke of Newcastle marched his army toward Howley Hall and demanded that Sir John surrender at once in the king's name. Although his kinsman, Thomas, was also a Royalist, Sir John was a stubborn man and refused to give up the Hall and its lands to anyone, whether Royalist or Roundhead. The result was that the Duke placed Howley Hall under siege.

Sir John, together with a young officer and a few servants, was successful in holding off Newcastle's troops for several days. At length the Duke rolled up his artillery and shot portions of the Hall to pieces, destroying the exquisite mullion tracery and many of the manor's fine furnishings. After the bombardment, Newcastle and his men looted the ruined Hall and killed a number of its defenders. The gatekeeper, who finally opened the door to the Duke's soldiers, was hacked to pieces on the spot, and Sir John and the young officer were imprisoned in a castle nearby.

Although parts of the Hall had been destroyed, enough of it was left intact to serve as a summer retreat in later decades for various families, among them the Villiers. Baron Villiers, the head of the family, traveled north each spring to the Hall for the shooting. One Palm Sunday when the family was there, Lady Anne Villiers, a relative of the baron's, left the Hall and walked to a nearby spring where she meant to swim. Whether she was startled by something or slipped by accident and fell into the spring, no one knows. In any case, she was knocked unconscious and drowned. After that, the spring became known as "Lady Anne's Well," and it is not far from Howley Hall Golf Club. Some people are convinced that it is often the ghost of Lady Anne that walks abroad over the haunted links.

Also very near the links is a winding road known as Scotchman's Lane. It is said to be named after the victim of a brutal murder by a highwayman, William Nevison, about the year 1670. The victim was a Scottish innkeeper named Fletcher. Fletcher recognized Nevison as he entered his tavern and decided to get help and try to capture the noted outlaw.

Slipping out the back of the inn, Fletcher took Nevison's equally famous horse, Brown Bess, and locked her in the stable. Then he struck out across the moors toward Howley Hall to summon the constables. Back at the inn, Nevison, suspicious of Fletcher's long absence, went outside and caught sight of Fletcher just as he was disappearing over the moors. Realizing what the innkeeper was up to, he bounded after him in hot pursuit. Catching up with him in the winding lane, Nevison stabbed the innkeeeper to death with a knife.

After the murder, Nevison returned to the stable, freed Brown Bess, and sped to York. He reached that town by midday and immediately showed himself on the bowling green to establish an alibi that he had been in York at the time of the murder. It did not work, however, for some time later Nevison was arrested and subsequently hanged at York Castle for his crime.

A number of local residents claim it is frequently the phantom of the brutally murdered Fletcher who wanders over the greens of Howley Hall golf links. Others say the ghosts are those of the gatekeeper, Lady Anne, or other persons who met sudden deaths in the region long ago. But two things remain certain—they are still being seen, and they are still unexplained.

The case is a purely visual one. No sounds ever accompany the apparitions, and there is no attendant movement that would indicate poltergeist activity. But there is little agreement by witnesses as to who the apparitions represent, for the acts of violence occurred so long ago. Yet it may be perfectly possible that they are the phantom-victims of those earlier days who feel compelled to remain earthbound to haunt the places of their deaths.

THE ARMY-NAVY STORE POLTERGEIST

WHILE A POLTERGEIST ACTIVITY NORMALLY CENTERS around one or more adolescents who are somehow disturbed, this poltergeist case involved no youngsters at all. Rather, it focused around two grown men who were veterans of World War II. Furthermore, the objects affected by disturbances were not the usual flying crockery and overturned chairs, but apparently several pairs of Army boots that were heard to "walk" all by themselves.

In the early 1950s, an Army veteran living in Lancashire, England, decided to go into business for himself. His name was Tom Sharp, and he had a friend, George Kempton, who owned a small Army-Navy surplus war goods shop. Tom knew that George was thinking of selling the shop, and he made him an offer for it. George readily accepted Tom's offer, a bill of sale for the premises was drawn up, and George said that he would hand over the store keys to Tom on the coming Friday. It was then Wednesday, and George said that he wanted to spend the next day tidying up the shop so that Tom could take it over.

When Tom, the new owner, showed up on Friday, he noticed that George was very nervous, and that he seemed to be having second thoughts about letting Tom run the business. It was not, said George, that he had any regrets about selling the shop; indeed, he had decided to retire. Well, then, argued Tom, why was he suddenly so reluctant to let it go?

"Because of a queer thing that happened yesterday while I was readying up the shop for you," answered George. "When you take over I don't want you to have any trouble like that."

"What trouble?" queried Tom. "Go on, tell me. I'm a good listener."

George's story was strange, and there was no mistake about it. He said that, as he had been preparing the shop for Tom, he had heard odd noises coming from the big room over the shop. It had sounded to him as though a man were clomping around up there. George said he was certain that no one was up there; he had seen no one go up nor had he hired any help to go up there to check over surplus stock. The upstairs room was used as a storeroom.

However, George told Tom, as the day went on the clomping footsteps grew increasingly louder. It sounded as if whoever was walking around up in the storeroom was becoming larger and heavier. By the end of the afternoon, the stamping footsteps sounded like those of a giant.

"Then what happened, George?" asked Tom anxiously.

"Well," answered George, "when it came time to catch my train home, I was only too glad to go, believe me!"

However, George continued, just as he was leaving the shop, he remembered that he'd left his coat on the upper floor when he'd gone up there early in the morning for something. He hesitated about going back up for it because of the ominous footsteps. But he started for the stairway anyway. As he did so, a violent shuddering crash rocked the whole building. This was enough for George, and he immediately bolted from the shop.

George's story perplexed Tom. He had known George for some years; he had been a commando during the war and had participated in some of the heaviest combat in World War II. It was hard for Tom to imagine such a man running from some strange noises. Perhaps it was a delayed reaction from his war service, and George was finally losing his nerve. Perhaps it was a good thing that he'd decided to retire.

But Tom was soon to discover that whatever was stamping about on the upper floor could hardly be explained as a case of nerves.

At any rate, George handed over the keys of the shop and wished Tom good luck. For the next few days nothing out of the ordinary happened, and Tom was glad to see that business was brisk. But one night as he was working late, he distinctly heard the steady, unfaltering tread of footsteps coming from the upstairs floor. Tom knew for a fact that there was no one in the shop but himself. He went outside to see whether anyone was outside. But there was no one at all.

"I was determined," he told a reporter later, "to find out what was going on, and I started to run up the stairs. As I reached the third step, my legs seemed suddenly to freeze. I looked up and sensed, more than saw, a figure walking along the small passageway at the top of the stairs. I admit that I was really frightened!"

When Tom opened up the store the following morning, he was astonished to find the place in great disarray. Strewn all over the floor were many pairs of thick-soled army boots. Only the previous afternoon he had neatly stacked them according to size on the shelves. At first Tom concluded that a burglar, after money in the cash register, had broken in. Finding only some loose change there, he'd probably revenged himself on the owner by throwing the boots about. But Tom changed his mind when he checked all the windows

and the back door. They were still firmly locked. There was clearly no way an intruder could have gotten into the shop.

Next morning the same scene met his eyes. Dozens of pairs of army boots had been dumped all over the floor indiscriminately. It was then that Tom began to connect the unnerving "walking" on the upper floor—which George had heard—with the boots being pulled down from the shelves and scattered about. During George's proprietorship, many pairs of the boots had been stored in the upstairs room. On many mornings after that the same thing happened, and Tom spent a good portion of his time picking up the scattered boots.

One night Tom had a good deal of bookkeeping work to catch up on, and he stayed at the shop long after the closing hour. As he sat hunched over the accounts, he was suddenly shocked to feel the light touch of a hand on his shoulder. Tom whirled around in his chair, but he could see nobody there. Yet he did hear sounds of fading footsteps.

Tom had talked about his troubles with a number of people, and eventually the newspapers got wind of the "walking boots" at the Army-Navy store. A number of reporters from one of the Lancashire papers got permission from Tom to stay all night in the shop and observe anything that might occur. They assured him that there must be some perfectly logical explanation for the strange goings-on. Perhaps rats or other small animals were getting into the shop and doing the damage. That evening the newsmen made a thorough search of the upstairs room and found it totally empty. Since he was wary of going up to this room—especially after dark—Tom had not been using it for storage for some time. The newsmen also checked the premises for rat holes, loose boards, and noisy shutters. But everything seemed in order.

One of the newsmen later wrote, "Throughout the evening, we heard a great variety of sounds, especially heavy bumping and thumping sounds. At other times there were noises like metal scraping the floor. It was just after midnight when we seemed to hear the sound of a chain being rattled across the floor. By this time we were all quite nervous. We were convinced that we were not hearing rats and mice, nor the antics of some jokester."

The reporters had been maintaining their vigil in the upstairs room but, after the midnight disturbances, they descended to the comparative quiet of the shop below. As the newsmen dozed or fitfully tried to sleep, they continued to hear noises from above. At dawn they conducted another search of the storage area on the upper floor. In the corner of the room they were astonished to find a long chain lying on the floor. None of them had seen it when they had searched the room the previous evening. When one of the reporters opened a closet door, he called his colleagues to come and take a look. A broken three-legged chair, which all had seen the evening before hanging on one of the wall pegs, was now hanging on another peg some distance away. At this point, the newsmen got into a squabble, each accusing the other of having come up during the night to move the chair.

While the argument continued over which of them had tried to "play ghost," Tom Sharp arrived at the shop and settled the debate. Tom swore on his word of honor that when he had left the shop the previous afternoon, there had been no chair on the upper floor. Moreover, he claimed, he had never seen that particular chair before in his life.

After the newsmen's overnight adventures, the poltergeist activity resumed its regular course—throwing Tom's merchandise about. The morning after the reporters had left, Tom arrived at the shop to find more of a mess than usual. Not only were the army boots scattered about, but boxes were upended spilling their contents, pants legs were tied together in knots, and shirts were unpinned and draped over counters and shelves. To Tom's despair, the activity continued for several more weeks; however, it then mercifully tapered off and then ceased altogether.

During the heyday of the poltergeist activity, a noted English clairvoyant—a psychic gifted with ability to perceive objects or matters beyond the five senses—visited the haunted Army-Navy shop and later told reporters that he had "seen" a number of beings inhabiting the building. All of these entities, he claimed, told of a tragedy or some injustice done them that kept their spirits earthbound. Later, an investigation conducted by psychical researchers and others interested in the case revealed that Tom's shop had been built on the site of an old jail. Down in the basement, an unused area was discovered to be paved with flagstones; it contained an old room that may have once been one of the cells.

Although the case was chiefly one of poltergeist disturbances, it contained other elements as well. There were apparitions witnessed during the course of it, and, when Tom Sharp felt the ghostly hand on his shoulder, it also qualified as a tactile case.

THE BIG GRAY MAN OF BEN MACDHUI

THE SECOND HIGHEST MOUNTAIN IN GREAT BRITAIN IS THE lofty Ben Macdhui in the southwestern part of Aberdeen in Scotland. Situated on the border of Banff County, its name means "mountain of the black pig" in Gaelic. Ben Macdhui is one of the six main peaks of the Cairngorm chain, and its upper slopes are bleak and almost bare of any vegetation. From its summit the view is a breathtaking one, encompassing Moray Firth, the hills of Caithness and Sutherland, Ben Nevis, Ben More in Perth County, and other peaks.

Ben Macdhui is also said to be haunted. Many eyewitnesses over the years have attested to the existence of a curious and frightening specter there, known locally as the "Big Gray Man of Ben Macdhui." However, the outward aspect of the phantom and the manner in which people have come in contact with it have been extremely diverse. Sometimes it has only been heard and not seen. At other times, only its presence has been felt—but strongly and unmistakably.

In 1914 a veteran mountain-climber and an honorary sheriff of Aberdeen named George Duncan reported seeing the large specter. At dusk as he was coming off the mountain and was driving along the Derry Road, he suddenly saw a tall figure in a black robe. It stood on an outcrop of rock several yards above him and seemed to be waving its long arms threateningly. Duncan felt a quivering stab of fear go up and down his spine. He instinctively gave his automobile more gas and was glad when he rounded a bend in the road and could see the figure no longer.

One of the earliest reports of the ghost—an auditory one—was in 1891. It was given by a chemistry professor, Norman Collie, who was a much-respected Fellow of the Royal Society and a scientist who took little stock in talk of ghosts. He was returning from the rocky cairn landmark at the summit late one afternoon when he distinctly heard footsteps not far behind him. Collie looked back as he continued on his way, but there were swirling mists that day and he saw nothing. He stopped for a few seconds to listen. The footsteps were getting closer and from the sound of them, he later reported, the strides of whoever was following him were much longer than his own. At this point, Collie panicked and began to run pell-mell downward through the mist-drenched boulders. He reeled along blindly for several miles until he saw the Rothiemurchus woods ahead. It was only then that he realized the terrifying footsteps were no longer following him.

A somewhat similar experience happened to a couple of

amateur naturalists, the two Welsh brothers, in 1904. They
were spending two weeks camping near the cairn landmark
at the summit of Ben Macdhui, collecting specimens of spi-
ders and various alpine flowers. During their first few nights
on the mountain, both brothers heard soft footsteps which
seemed to be following them about. However, they never
saw anything to account for the footfalls. Then, as the days
went by, they began to hear the footsteps during daylight
hours as well. They were also distinctly aware at times of
some "presence" standing beside them. But never did the
brothers see anything to account for it.

In the late 1920s, the well-known psychic Joan Grant and
her physician husband were strolling along in the Rothiemurchus woods. It was a bright sunny day, and they were
headed toward the Cairngorms. Suddenly a strange feeling
of stark terror gripped Joan. Grabbing her husband by the
arm, she practically dragged him back down the path they
had taken through the woods. Later she said she was certain
that something "utterly malign, four-legged and obscenely
human, invisible and yet solid" was trying to get to her.
Several months later a friend of her father's declared that he
had had an almost identical experience in the same part of
the Rothiemurchus woods.

Early in World War II, a Scottish naturalist named Wendy
Wood was walking near the entrance to Lairig Ghru pass.
After hours of searching for specimens on the lower slopes
of Ben Macdhui, she was about ready to call it a day and go
back down the mountain. Night was fast coming on, and a
light snow lay on the ground. Then all at once she heard a
voice "of gigantic resonance" right beside her. To Wendy it
sounded like the Gaelic of the Scottish Highlands, but so
startled and terrified was she that she could not really make
out any words. Getting hold of herself finally, she reasoned

that it may have been an echo or the bleat of a lost sheep or something of that kind that she had heard. Then she heard the loud garbled voice shout again—right at her feet. Though still terrified, Wendy again tried to think clearly. The idea came to her that perhaps someone was lying injured in the snow quite close to her. So she began to walk in widening concentric circles to see if she could discover the owner of the voice.

When she was satisfied that no one was anywhere around her, Wendy felt cold fear take possession of her. She turned and started to flee down the mountain. It was then that she heard the heavy crunching footsteps behind her. They seemed to follow her own quickening footsteps through the snow. She had the clear impression that whoever or whatever the pursuer was, it was just behind her. At one point in her flight, she thought that possibly she was hearing the echoes of her own footfalls. But when she realized her own rapid steps were not in time with the ponderous crunching sounds behind her, sheer terror seized Wendy. In a frenzy of fear, she clawed and stumbled her way down the remaining slopes until, near the village of Whitewell, the bark of a sheep dog brought her back to reality. With infinite relief, she could no longer hear the heavy crunching steps behind her.

One October afternoon in 1943, another experienced mountain-climber and naturalist, Alexander Tewnion, was out climbing all by himself. As he reached the cairn at the summit, a heavy blanket of mist rolled across the Lairig Ghru and settled over the entire mountain. As the wind began to rise, the atmosphere grew dank and thick with moisture. Tewnion, fearing that a storm was coming on, decided to make his way back down by the Coire Etchachan pathway. On his way downward, he suddenly heard a loud footstep behind him, then another and another. Through

the wind, he could hear that they were spaced out at long intervals—much longer than his own—as if they were those of a very large man. Then, remembering that he had a revolver, he paused and tried to peer through the jagged sheets of whirling mist. All of a sudden, he saw an enormous shape loom up before him, recede a little way, then charge straight at him. Tewnion quickly drew his revolver and fired three rounds at the huge figure. When it still advanced toward him, Tewnion turned tail and dashed headlong down the path, not looking behind him. As he later told it, he reached the town of Glen Derry "in a time I have never bettered!"

Some months before Tewnion's experience, a war veteran named Sydney Scroggie was out walking near the Shelter Stone on Ben Macdhui. He was alone, and dusk was starting to fall. Happening to look down on Loch Etchachan below him, he suddenly saw a tall human figure step out of the darkness on one side of the lake. Clearly silhouetted against the water, it walked with long and measured steps across some small creeks and then vanished in the darkness at the other end of the lake. Curious, Scroggie decided to investigate and soon reached the spot where the figure had walked. He looked about but could see no one, nor could he discover any footprints where they ought to have been. Scroggie called out to see if anyone would answer, but all he could hear was the echo of his own words coming back from the Highlands. Nervously aware of the approaching darkness and the brooding silence all about him, Scroggie made his way back to his camp.

Such were only a few of the experiences of witnesses to the so-called Big Gray Man of Macdhui. Evaluated in terms of psychical research, it would certainly qualify as an apparitional case, even though the descriptions of the abnormally large phantom or phantoms were—due to the fright of the observers—sketchy. Yet in many of the auditory experiences, it also belongs more properly in the poltergeistic realm. Further, all of these experiences were somewhat rare in that they occurred out of doors in remote and lonely spots of the Scottish Highlands. Finally, these phenomena seem to have a permanency about them—as if they were to continue.

THE GHOSTS OF BORLEY RECTORY

THE LATE ENGLISH PSYCHICAL RESEARCHER HARRY PRICE once called the Borley Rectory case "the most fully documented of poltergeist infestation in the history of psychical research." Price knew all about it—he himself was chiefly responsible for unearthing many new angles in this celebrated case. The Borley story also had eerie visual effects, among them the famous Nun of Borley Rectory, who was seen on several occasions. There were reportedly over two hundred firsthand witnesses to the phenomena in and around the old building. In any event, no case in psychic literature has been more written about, argued over, or referred to than this one.

The Rectory—gutted and destroyed by fire in 1939—with its nearby twelfth-century church stood about sixty miles north of London on a gloomy isolated knoll surrounded by trees. Constructed of red brick, it was a two-storied Victorian monstrosity with some thirty high-ceilinged rooms, drafty corridors, rambling cellars, heavy gables, and a garden which had long since gone to seed. It was built in the early 1860s by the Reverend Henry Bull, reputedly on the foundation stones of two buildings that had previously stood there. When Bull died in 1892, his son Harry took over as rector. He remained so until 1927, when he himself died. After that the Bull family had difficulty in finding a new rector because the house, in addition to being remote, had neither electricity nor gas, and water had to be pumped by hand. Several clergymen refused the post when it was offered to them. At length, the Reverend G. Eric Smith and his wife accepted the position and went to live there in 1927. The couple moved out again the following summer, not so much because of the lack of modern facilities but because of the strange things that were occurring there.

One morning, for instance, when Mrs. Smith was cleaning out a cupboard in the library, she came across a brown paper parcel neatly tied with a string. Untying it, she was shocked to discover a small human skull in perfect condition. Later, a doctor friend said it was the skull of a young woman. No one knew to whom it belonged, where it had come from, or how it had got into the cupboard. One rectory workman claimed it had been in the house for some time, but finally it had been taken out of the house and buried. So Reverend Smith reburied the grisly relic in the churchyard nearby.

Shortly after the Smiths moved into the house, very odd things began to happen. Bells rang of their own accord. Keys would fly out of their locks. Strange lights were seen to flicker in vacant rooms. Once when Smith was alone in the house, he heard shrill whisperings over his head—noises

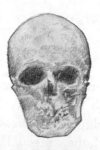

which followed him as he walked about the house. Another time he heard a woman's voice pleading pitifully, "Don't, Carlos, don't!" Mrs. Smith also heard soft moanings and mutterings, and frequently saw a shadowy figure leaning over one of the rectory gates. Whenever she approached it, the figure instantly vanished. This, one of the maids told her, might well be the celebrated Nun of Borley Rectory. She had herself, she said, witnessed one of the phenomena for which the Rectory was noted—a large black coach drawn by two horses. The girl said she had seen it gallop through the hedge, sweep across the lawn, and then vanish. And she too, she declared, had seen the "nun" leaning wistfully over one of the rectory gates.

It was not long before the Smiths learned the legend connected with the nun. Reputedly, she had been a beautiful young novice who belonged to a nunnery at Bures, a town about seven miles from Borley, in the thirteenth century. At that time there was supposed to have been a monastery at Borley, and the nun had fallen in love with one of the lay brothers there. One day they arranged to elope, and another brother had a coach waiting in the woods behind the monastery where the couple frequently met. According to one version of the story, the couple made their escape in a black coach drawn by two bay horses. However, their superiors got wind of their elopement and gave chase. They were caught and a horrible punishment followed. The would-be bridegroom was either hanged or beheaded. The bride-to-be was said to have been bricked up alive—either in her own convent or somewhere at Borley monastery. Such was the story behind the apparitions of the nun and the black coach with its horses.

But as Harry Price and others later pointed out, the story has plenty of historical holes in it. For one thing, there is no evidence that a monastery ever existed in former times at Borley, nor was there ever a nunnery at Bures. Further, the type of large coach seen by witnesses was not invented until the early fifteenth century, and even then they were used only by noblemen and women of the first rank. Lastly, there is no evidence that English nuns were ever walled up alive— no matter how serious their crime.

Nevertheless, the apparitional nun cannot be lightly dismissed as a hallucination, for she had been seen on the grounds by numerous witnesses, many of them cultured and intelligent people. Price himself talked to some seventeen persons who, alone or together, saw her phantom. And some of these also saw the coach and horses.

While the nun was never seen far from the rectory, she was never seen indoors. Usually, observers caught sight of her on a long path next to a stone wall on the lawn, known as the Nun's Walk. On the other side of the lawn, facing the walk, is the summer house; it was erected by Henry Bull for the sole purpose of watching for the spectral lady. He and his son Harry were in the habit of spending hours there, smoking their pipes, just watching out for her. It was the elder Bull who ordered the main window of the dining room bricked up, for the nun frequently used to stare in at the family while they were eating, her face close to the glass. The famous nun was seen at all times of the day—at dawn, dusk, in daylight, and even in brilliant sunlight at noontime.

One of Harry Price's most interesting interviews was with the surviving daughters of Harry Bull, who once encountered the nun in full sunlight. On a summer day in 1900, three of the Bull sisters were returning from a party and, upon entering the rectory grounds, saw a young woman in the garb of a nun. She was saying her beads, and her head was bowed. As the three girls watched, the nun half walked, half glided along the Nun's Walk. One of the girls ran to fetch another sister, and soon all four of them stood by the summer house staring fascinated at the ghostly nun. Then one of the sisters made a movement as if to approach the figure. The phantom stopped, turned to face the group, and promptly vanished. One of the Bull sisters recalled, "There was an expression of intense grief on her face." Price later wrote, "For an apparently solid, three-dimensional objective ghost to be seen simultaneously by four people, in sunlight, is concrete evidence that cannot be explained away."

During the long time they lived in the rectory, the Bull family saw and heard many strange phenomena. Once Harry Bull saw a little wizened old man standing on the lawn, his features plainly visible. He recognized him as "Old Amos," a family servant who had died some two hundred years before. How? Because this retainer had been one of the family's favorite characters, an eccentric gardener, stories of whose appearance had been handed down from one generation of Bulls to another.

To the Bulls, bell-ringing, tramping footsteps, rappings— all came to be common occurrences in their lives. So were ghostly shapes of many kinds. One day the Bull sisters saw a girl dressed in white walking toward a nearby river. Then she just vanished. One night Edith Bull, one of the sisters, met a tall dark man in one of the rectory passageways. He too vanished. On more than one occasion Harry Bull had witnessed the celebrated black coach and bays. Another time he saw a pair of legs move behind a thicket. When the figure emerged, it was headless! The apparition then passed right through a closed gate, was seen to drift across the garden, then faded from view.

Edward Cooper and his wife, employed by the Bull family for decades, witnessed many odd things at the rectory. They told Harry Price of one incident when they were residing in a nearby cottage in 1916. In early spring, they heard sounds like those of a large dog padding about the kitchen. These continued for some months. Then one evening they heard a thunderous crash coming from the kitchen, as if all their plates and dishes were being broken to smithereens. Dashing into the kitchen with a lit candle, they discovered not so much as a cup had been broken. Curiously, from that moment forward, they never heard the padding dog again. The couple also observed the apparition of the nun many times, usually gliding across the road or crossing the courtyard. And early one morning in 1919, as they were talking in bed, Mr. and Mrs. Cooper saw a tiny black shape of a man running about their bedroom. When Cooper got out of bed, it instantly vanished.

On one bright moonlit night, Cooper was preparing to go to bed when he glanced out the window of his bedroom and saw lights swiftly approaching his cottage. However, they seemed to be in the church meadow, not on the road, and he asked himself why they would be coming from out there. As he stared at the lights, Cooper suddenly realized he was looking into the headlamps of an old-fashioned coach being pulled by two bay horses. Seated on the box were two figures wearing top hats. Awestruck, he gaped as the coach swept on through the hedge, across the road, and into the farmyard. It had made no noise and had *passed through* every obstacle in its way.

Another strange story was told to Harry Price by a carpenter named Fred Cartwright, who was repairing some buildings near the rectory in the fall of 1927. At the time, no one was living at the manor; Harry Bull had recently died and the Smiths had not yet moved in. Every morning Cartwright would pass the rectory just as it was becoming daylight. On the second morning of his job, he was passing one of the gates of the rectory drive when he saw a woman in the habit of a Sister of Mercy standing there. She did not look unusual in any way, and Cartwright, vaguely wondering what she was waiting for, passed by and on to his work. Three days later, at the same spot, he saw the nun again; she appeared fatigued and her eyes were closed. New to the area, Cartwright knew nothing of the Borley hauntings and had no suspicions that the figure was a phantom. The third time he saw her was nearly a week later, at the same time and place. Again the nun's eyes were closed, and this time she appeared not only tired but ill as well. After he had passed by, Cartwright decided to ask her if she needed help; turning to do so, he saw that she had vanished. The carpenter thought she must have gone inside the rectory.

The fourth and final time Cartwright saw the nun was on the following Friday morning. She was standing in her usual place by the gate and the carpenter decided he'd say "Good morning" to her. But before he got to the gate she was gone. Cartwright said he did not exactly see her disappear; one moment she was there, the next she was not. He then opened the gate and searched about for her, but he could find no trace. When he told the story to some local citizens, he learned that his meetings had been with none other than the famous Nun of Borley Rectory.

It was only a few months after Cartwright's experience that the Smiths came to live at Borley. In addition to the poltergeist activity, they found the rectory cold, depressing, and difficult to run without the help of servants. Shutting off most of the rooms, they tried to make the best of things. It was during that winter of 1928–29 that they regularly heard the ghostly whisperings, dragging footsteps, and other disturbances. With the coming of spring, Borley Rectory suddenly made big news throughout Britain. A reporter for the London *Daily Mirror*, a Mr. A. V. Wall, wrote a sensational piece about the odd occurrences at the rectory. Wall omitted none of the grisly details of the nun's legend, the ghostly black coach, the ominous footsteps, or any other of the juicy tales connected with the place. In a follow-up piece, Wall further whetted his readers' appetites when he wrote that England's noted ghost-hunter, Harry Price, had agreed to investigate the Borley hauntings. Price, as everyone interested in psychic matters knew, was Director of the National Laboratory of Psychical Research; he was also the author of the best-selling *Poltergeist Over England,* in which he recounted many of his personal investigations.

Price, delighted with the prospect of probing the Borley disturbances, sallied forth immediately to the rectory, accompanied by Wall. His first day there was a ghost-hunter's dream come true. As he and Wall were standing by the summer house in the early evening, Wall declared that he saw a ghostly figure gliding along the Nun's Walk. Price thought he saw it, too, but he could not be certain. Returning to the house under the glass-roofed veranda, the two men were suddenly showered with glass splinters as a brick came crashing through the roof, landing only a few inches from them. Previously, they had sealed off all doors and windows that they could not watch personally. Reentering the house, they searched the whole rectory again and found all the seals in place. As they descended the stairs to the main hall, a glass candlestick came hurtling down after them and smashed at their feet. Later they were pelted with a flurry of mothballs, pebbles, pieces of slate, and other objects. Still later the servants' bells rang all by themselves. Wall and Price could see their pull-cords moving up and down. "We could find no explanation," wrote Price subsequently, "of these truly poltergeist phenomena."

As midnight approached, Price decided to hold a seance in the Blue Room of the rectory. He had deliberately chosen this room, for both Harry Bull and his father had died there. Price hoped to contact their spirits and perhaps gain more information about the disturbances. Using the table-rapping method, Price was soon rewarded by an entity coming through claiming to be "the late Harry Bull." During the seance various rappings and thumpings were heard. At last, after no more significant information was received through Bull—other than the fact that he claimed to be present in spirit—the seance broke up. Harry Price later wrote, "A day to be remembered, even by an experienced investigator. Although I have investigated many haunted houses, before and since, never have such phenomena impressed me as they did on this historic day. Sixteen hours of thrills!"

Price visited the rectory many times in 1929 and was present with the Smiths during many weird happenings. For long periods of time, for example, every bell in the house would peal incessantly. Showers of pebbles and keys came from nowhere. By mid-July the Smiths, finding it impossible to live there anymore, moved to a nearby town. However, they returned from time to time and kept Price informed about the on-going poltergeist activity. Once-secured windows were found wide open. Furniture was discovered tossed about. Once part of a fireplace was removed and the stones found piled up on the staircase.

After the departure of the Smiths, Borley remained vacant for some months; it was not until October 1930 that a new rector could be found. Wrote Price, "Then came the Foysters—and pandemonium! The poltergeists excelled themselves!" The new rector was Reverend Lionel Foyster who, with his wife Marianne and two young children, bravely took up residence at Borley. Price described the family as a charming and gracious one, but wrote that he "felt sorry" for them. He had good reason to, for the poltergeists lost no time in exhibiting their bag of tricks. The wonder is how the Foysters stayed one week in the house, let alone the five years they actually did. On their very first day, a disembodied voice started calling, "Marianne! Marianne!" Objects disappeared, then reappeared.

During their long stay, the Foysters witnessed hundreds of odd and sometimes vicious phenomena. Marianne often saw the wraith of "Harry Bull" materialize in a gray dressing gown at various locations in the house. It was a miracle the family did not go out of their minds with the constant bell-ringing alone. Cryptic messages on little pieces of paper in a childish hand appealing to "Marianne" for "help" would flutter down from the ceilings. Similar messages would be found scribbled on the walls. Strange odors of lavender perfume and the smell of cooking—when no meals were being prepared—would often permeate the rectory. Pieces of heavy iron and stones were hurled at the rector and his wife. Oddly, sometimes the poltergeists were actually helpful, returning lost articles in easy-to-find places. Once a pile of hymnbooks was found in the kitchen—at a time when the church was very short of them!

But with the passage of nearly a year, the poltergeist activity grew positively ugly. One evening, Marianne was struck a savage blow under the eye, resulting in a cut that bled copiously; her eye remained black for several days. Pins with their points up were found in chairs. "Traps"—piles of dishes, a floor polisher, boxes, and other obstacles—were laid for them so that they would trip or stumble and hurt themselves. Meanwhile, queer messages were still found deposited around the house with such requests as "Marianne help me." Once Marianne wrote under one of these notes, "What do you want?" and left it in a prominent place. Next day the paper bore the cryptic reply: "Rest."

After a year of enduring these events, Foyster determined to hold the rites of exorcism, complete with the sprinkling of holy water about the premises. All he got for his trouble was a stone—as big as a man's fist—flung at him. It hit him on the shoulder and caused much pain. Determined to try again, he

obtained the aid of three other clergymen. These four par-
sons, armed with incense and holy water, did a thorough job
of blessing and sprinkling the entire rectory from attic to
cellar. At first, it seemed their combined efforts had done the
trick. But later that day there was a flurry of stone-throwing
and the clanging of every bell in the house. Next day a whole
batch of clean linen was dragged from a closet and trailed
across the floor.

The disturbances intensified in the weeks that followed.
Once the spirit of Harry Bull manifested itself to Marianne
and another time a heavy flatiron was hurled at her. Pepper
was found strewn over beds. Bells clanged unnervingly.
Pieces of brick would drop by the rector's plate while he was
eating. A pottery fragment hit his wife on one occasion,
causing blood to flow. Kitchen utensils were tossed about.
Fire started in an empty room upstairs (it was put out before
it spread). At the height of the phenomena in 1931, a friend
again attempted exorcism; that night Marianne was flung
out of her bed three times. Pleading messages, appealing to
Marianne for help, continued to float down from the ceilings
and were scribbled in a shaky hand on walls.

By the autumn of 1935, the long-suffering Foysters had
had enough. They had "stuck it" at the rectory for five
poltergeist-ridden years. In October they moved out, sick
and weary of the ordeal they had so long endured. The
rectorship stood vacant for several months until the Reverend A. C. Henning accepted the post. Harry Price, of course,
still maintained his interest in the place, and it was Henning
who informed him that Borley could be leased to a layman.
Intrigued, Price rented the estate for a year, starting in the
spring of 1937. The Reverend Henning continued to live
there as rector.

Thus began one of the biggest ghost hunts in the history

of psychical research. Price himself—whose home was 150 miles distant—could not live at Borley all the time, so he advertised in the London *Times* for volunteer ghost-hunters. He wished to keep the place under surveillance night and day, under scientific conditions imposed by himself. Volunteers would live at the rectory and work in shifts around the clock, observing odd events and keeping records. Soon Price had handpicked about forty such persons, including engineers, scientists, doctors, military officers, and other professional men and women. All would pitch in to solve, as Price put it, "The Great Borley Mystery."

What this corps of observers witnessed at the rectory would fill a book of many pages, and only a sampling can be given here. One woman observer saw the phantasmal nun three separate times. A mysterious "cold spot" was found just outside the Blue Room where people felt their flesh become chilled. Rappings, knockings, and dragging footsteps were regularly heard by everyone. Several observers reported being touched or stroked by unseen hands. Peculiar odors were smelled and odd luminosities were seen in windows from the outside. Doors locked and unlocked. Bells chimed madly. Many new scribblings appeared on the walls.

In May of 1938, Harry Price's lease—and with it his investigation—ended. The new owner of Borley Rectory, which he renamed The Priory, was a Captain W. H. Gregson of the Royal Engineers, who moved in just before Christmas, 1938. Far from being disturbed by the tales of the hauntings, Gregson thought it all "added charm to the place." Actually, the intensity of the disturbances seemed to wane after he and his two sons took up residence at Borley. But they did not cease by any means. Strange footsteps were still heard and bells still chimed from time to time.

Then, just a few weeks later, on February 27, 1939, the

end of Borley Rectory came in a spectacular way. As the captain was arranging some books in the main hall, a lamp some distance away overturned, flooding the place with oil which soon ignited. Knowing he could do little alone, he phoned for the nearby Sudbury fire department. But by the time they arrived, the rectory was gutted and the roof had caved in. Even as the house burned that night, a constable claimed he saw "a lady and gentleman in cloaks" standing quite near Gregson, although the captain later insisted that nobody else was on the premises except himself and the firemen. Also during the blaze, villagers reported seeing two persons at the upper windows. One was described as a "young girl," the other as some kind of "formless shape."

The fire alone, however, failed to halt the apparitions at what was left of the old rectory. Approximately a month afterward, a young couple and a few friends were examining the blackened manor by moonlight. And there, standing on the Nun's Walk, they all saw "a small woman" in what was once the Blue Room upstairs. The figure approached the window, stood there for a few seconds, then turned toward a gutted wall and appeared to walk straight through it. The strange part of this story was that the woman must have been standing on nothing—in midair—because the floor of the Blue Room had collapsed in the fire.

So, for all practical purposes, ended the occurrences at Borley Rectory. Though he had reams of data, Harry Price could shed little explanatory light on them—he could only say that the occurrences had certainly taken place. And the ruined rectory continues to be called "the most haunted house in England."

THE
MIAMI
POLTERGEIST

IN RECENT YEARS, NO POLTERGEIST CASE HAS BEEN MORE
thoroughly documented than this one. Investigated by two
parapsychologists from the American Society of Psychical
Research—who were called in early—it occurred on the
premises of a small manufacturing company in Miami in
1966. In all, ASPR researchers catalogued no fewer than 224
separate events of poltergeist activity and even drew a detailed map of them.

Business had been going well at Tropication Arts, Inc., in
Miami, Florida, throughout 1966—until December of that
year. The small firm was a wholesale outfit for novelty and
souvenir items to the local tourist trade. Many of Tropication's gifts—glass beverage mugs, sailfish ashtrays, zombie
glasses, rubber daggers, small painted glasses, even bamboo
backscratchers—were imported from Hong Kong, Shang-

hai, Kowloon, and other places in the Far East. When they arrived at Tropication Arts, they were then painted by the company's three artists with such symbols of Florida as flamingos and palm trees. Before the merchandise was shipped to retail dealers, it had to be inventoried and stocked on shelves in a large storeroom. This room contained three sturdy tiers of shelving with four numbered aisles between and on either side of them. Clerks could walk through these wide aisles, picking and assembling orders for shipment.

The owners of Tropication Arts, Alvin Laubheim and Glen Lewis, were looking forward to an even brisker and more profitable year in 1967. Then, around December 15, weird things started happening at the company. There seemed to be an inordinate amount of breakage, especially among the amber glass steins. Laubheim and Lewis put this down to carelessness on the part of the shipping clerks, particulary a young Cuban refugee. His name was Julio Vasquez, and he always appeared to be in the vicinity when something got broken. The clerks were warned to be more careful, yet they protested that they were not causing the damage. It just seemed to happen, often when none of them were even within reaching distance of the merchandise.

As the days passed, however, these accidents increased. Cartons of plastic fans and rubber daggers would clatter to the floor when a worker's back was turned. Boxes of combs and glasses would be found on the floor in the morning that had not been seen during the previous day. Mugs would roll off the shelves and smash to bits. These were getting broken so fast that the firm's inventory threatened to run low. Finally, Mr. Laubheim instructed Julio and the other clerks to place the glass mugs on their sides with the handles down so that they would not roll or slide off the shelves.

Al Laubheim himself demonstrated this to his employees.

"Now," he said, "if you put them in this position, they're not going to break or fall . . ."

With that, Laubheim turned and walked away. He had not gone ten steps when one of the mugs he had just placed on its side came crashing down into the aisle. The mug had been at least eight inches from the edge of the shelf and none of his employees were closer than fifteen feet to it when it fell. Later that same day—it was now the second week in January—there was pandemonium in the Tropication store-room. Alligator ashtrays skittered off shelves and clattered into the aisles. More mugs smashed on the floor. Glasses shattered in the aisles. A carton of 100 backscratchers hit the floor with a loud cracking noise. "I realized then," declared Laubheim later, "that something was definitely wrong around the place."

It happened that the following day was Friday the thirteenth. Glen Lewis, who was not present at the business as often as his colleague, was told over the telephone about the baffling events. Exceedingly skeptical, he came over to Tropication Arts that afternoon for a personal inspection. Soon he was witnessing a spectacle that truly astonished him. Whole boxes of various merchandise left their shelves and fell to the floor before his eyes. Gaily painted zombie glasses and mugs teetered on their edges and tumbled into the aisles. Lewis stated later, "I would put some of the things back, but they would continue to fall off the shelves."

Well aware by now that they were up against something they could neither understand nor control, the owners decided to seek help. Many of the women employed by the company were scared out of their wits by the disheartening occurrences. Some even broke down and wept. Al Laubheim decided the police should be called, and his partner agreed. He made the call on Saturday, the fourteenth.

After talking with Al Laubheim, the desk sergeant at the
local precinct put down the phone and called Patrolman
William Killiam over to him. "Bill, I just talked with a man
who claims he has a ghost in his place of business . . . going
around breaking ashtrays and other stuff. He's probably
some kind of nut, but you'd better check it out anyway."

Only Al Laubheim and Julio were present at Tropication
Arts when Officer Killiam arrived. Conducted to the storeroom area, Killiam began looking down each of the aisles.

Halfway down Aisle 4, he was amazed to see a zombie glass fall from its shelf and break to bits on the floor. Neither he, the owner, nor Julio had been anywhere near it. Killiam had seen enough. He phoned to the precinct for help in investigating the strange case.

Inside an hour, two more officers and a sergeant arrived at Tropication Arts. By then four more events had occurred. A heavy cardboard tin in Tier 3 fell to the floor. Then the one next to it fell. Afterward a carton of pencil sharpeners toppled into Aisle 2. Julio replaced them, and five minutes later they fell to the floor again. A few minutes later, everyone present witnessed the next disturbance. A box of address books on Tier 2 was seen to float out into the aisle, as if lifted by invisible hands, and then to plummet straight down upon the floor, as if the invisible hands had suddenly released it. The box had been a good eight inches from the edge of the shelf. Before the perplexed officers departed, they tested the shelves to see if vibrations or other movements might be causing the items to fall. "We shook every one of them," Killiam said later, "and nothing fell at all."

With the departure of the officers, Laubheim sought help from another quarter. He telephoned an old friend named Brooks who was a professional magician and asked him to look into the strange goings-on. Brooks pooh-poohed his friend's problem at first. "My first reaction was that the clerks or somebody was playing a prank on him," reported Brooks later. Even so, he came over and spent more than an hour looking around. "I saw nothing happen and I discounted the whole thing. As a matter of fact, I made a practical joke out of it by showing them how—while I was standing talking to someone—I took an item from behind my back and threw it and they all jumped and said, 'There it goes again,' so I wasn't convinced."

Goodnaturedly Brooks agreed to come back for another look on Monday when everyone would be at work. About noontime that day, Brooks was thunderstruck when he saw two boxes of combs float out from the shelf into the air, then drop to the floor with a loud clatter. Even more amazing was that one box remained on top of the other; they moved out as a pair and stayed in that position when they came to rest. Brooks could see no way in which this event could have been staged, for Julio was on his go-cart in another aisle, and other workers were nowhere near the area. "I still don't buy this spook theory," he observed later, "but something did move those boxes, and I couldn't figure out what."

During the whole of the following week, owners and employees alike were kept busy picking things up off the storage room floor as fast as they fell. Zombie glasses, mugs, whole cartons of merchandise began to take new and bizarre angles of flight—sometimes swooping up into the air and even doing loop-the-loops before hurtling into the aisles. The strange force causing the events even started attacking the soft drinks that the employees were drinking on their breaks. Coke, Tab, and Orange Crush bottles would suddenly leave their resting places and sail through the air. Sometimes they were seen to bounce a number of times, as though an invisible basketball player were dribbling them.

For weeks the owners of the firm had been worried that news of the strange happenings would leak out and hurt their business. But inevitably word got out as deliverymen and other service people coming in and out saw odd things occurring. On January 11 the first newspaper reporter showed up; after that, TV cameramen and radio reporters began dropping in to try to film or report the happenings on the spot. Curiously, though, when TV camera crews attempted to televise the events, nothing happened.

As early as January 13, a popular writer on occult subjects had learned of the Miami poltergeist activity and paid a visit to Tropication Arts. After witnessing some of the events in the storage area, she contacted the American Society for Psychical Research and spoke to two parapsychologists associated with that organization. Delighted at the opportunity to study an on-going poltergeist case, they arrived at Tropication Arts the third week in January. The two researchers were not disappointed. They witnessed boxes of back-scratchers hurtle into the aisles, glass mugs leave their shelves and smash on the floor, and alligator ashtrays leave their tiers and sail through the air.

Trained to investigate poltergeist cases scientifically, the researchers set up a procedure for studying the effects of the odd force present in the storage room. They wanted to find out two things: first, whether or not there was fraud or trickery going on; second, whether the events were centering around any particular person or persons. Instead of simply waiting for isolated events to happen willynilly, they selected a number of target areas and placed target objects in them. For example, a small glass would be placed in target area B on Tier 2. The researchers could keep this specific object under observation much more easily than the whole big storage room. Then, when an event did take place involving, say, the glass, the observers had no doubt as to the origin of the movement, the distance the object traveled, who was near it, and other details.

The ASPR scientists spent the next ten days evaluating the case from every angle. Not only did they witness events as they occurred, but they also interviewed witnesses about events that had taken place before their arrival. By February 1, when the researchers left Miami, they had recorded a total of 224 separate events of poltergeist activity. Approximately one-third of these occurred while one or both of them were present.

Early in the case, the scientists observed that objects were most often disturbed in particular locations—around certain tiers and aisles—and they were therefore able to concentrate their attention on these areas. In many instances, objects were disturbed that had been placed in selected target areas, and these were kept under a careful watch. By the time they left Miami, the researchers had the answer to their first question: in no instance was evidence found that any of the events were caused by fraud or trickery. As for the answer to their second question, the following typical entry in one parapsychologist's notebook and later quoted in their report provides a clue:

At 2:09 P.M., a mug broke in Aisle 4. It came from target area A on Tier 3. The previous day, I had replaced the unbroken mug with one that had been damaged when the box of mugs fell to the floor. I had put it between the cowbell and a Fanta bottle, placing two small cartons in front of the three target objects. At 1:30 P.M., there had been a change; Julio asked if he might replace the broken mug with a new one because "maybe the ghost don't like the old one." I had carefully checked Julio's replacement and could discover nothing suspicious about it. When it left its place, clearing the objects in front, Julio, as so often before, was facing me. I was by the desk facing Aisle 3; two other persons were to my right. No one else was present. Julio was walking south in Aisle 3 with a broom in his hand. The mug moved in a northwesterly direction, its place of origin being four feet from Julio, and its direction of movement away from him.

For some time the two scientists had suspected that the events were somehow connected with the young Cuban.

Julio had been present or at least on the premises during every one of the occurrences. One day, when Julio had a cold and did not come to work, there had been no disturbances at all. And when Julio left his job at Tropication Arts on February 1—the same day the researchers left—the poltergeist activity ceased altogether.

As in so many poltergeist cases, noted the scientists, the events tended to center around an adolescent "focus person"—in this instance, Julio. The boy was doubtless troubled about something, either consciously or subconsciously. Whatever it was that was disturbing him—thus releasing psychic forces powerful enough to influence objects at a distance—the scientists never found out. After leaving his job, Julio dropped out of sight and was never heard from again.

THE YORKSHIRE MUSEUM PHANTOM

THIS CELEBRATED APPARITION CASE BEGAN IN THE FALL OF 1953 in the Yorkshire Museum, a little-known institution on Museum Street in York, England. This small museum would soon after be catapulted into the world's headlines by a series of occurrences so inexplicable as to become classics of occult literature.

The story started when the apparent ghost of a little gentleman, clad in Edwardian clothes, manifested itself to George L. Jonas, caretaker of the Yorkshire Museum. The date of this encounter was September 20, 1953, late on a Sunday night. That evening an evangelical meeting—one of several to come—was held in one of the main rooms of the museum. On duty that night were Mr. Jonas and his wife.

They did not live at the museum but were required to be present when the building was being used. After the religious gathering had finished, Mr. Jonas locked the front door and went to join his wife in the kitchen, which was in the basement of the building. She had been waiting there for him and now they were preparing to leave the museum and catch their bus for home.

At twenty minutes before midnight, both Jonas and his wife heard footsteps coming from the museum above them. Believing it was the institution's curator, Mr. Willmott, going into his office, Jonas went back upstairs to make sure of this. Also, he wanted to report to him that he was now going off duty.

"I went upstairs," said Mr. Jonas in a later statement to a reporter for the *Yorkshire Evening Press*, "to tell him we were ready to leave. I fully expected to see him, but when I was halfway up the stairs I saw an elderly man crossing from Mr. Willmott's office into another room. I thought he was an odd-looking chap because he was wearing a frock coat, drainpipe trousers, and had fluffy side-whiskers. He had very little hair and walked with a slight stoop."

Jonas decided the man must be some kind of eccentric professor. As he neared the top of the stairs, the man seemed to change his mind, turn, and walk back into the office. When Jonas got to the door, the man once more appeared to change his mind and turned quickly to come out.

"I stood to one side," Jonas continued, "to let him pass and said, 'Excuse me, sir, are you looking for Mr. Willmott?' He did not answer but just shuffled past me and began to go down the stairs toward the library. Being only a few feet from him, I saw his face clearly and could pick him out from a photograph any time. He looked agitated, had a frown on his face, and kept muttering: 'I must find it; I must find it.'"

Jonas said that it was a queer experience, but that he did not think about ghosts for one minute. "He looked just as real as you or me," he went on. "But I did not want him running around so late at night, and anyway I wanted to lock up and catch my bus. As I followed him down the stairs, I noticed that he was wearing what seemed to be elastic-sided boots, and I remember thinking how old-fashioned the big black buttons looked on the back of his coat."

Next, the caretaker said, the elderly man, still muttering, went into the library. It was in darkness, and Jonas switched on the lights as he followed just a few yards behind the figure. Jonas then saw the man stand between two tall book racks and start to pull first one book, then another from the shelves. The strange man seemed to want to find something.

The caretaker continued his story: "I thought to myself, this has gone far enough. So, thinking he was deaf, I stretched my hand out to touch him on the shoulder. But as my hand drew near his coat he vanished, and the book he had been holding dropped to the floor." Jonas bent down and picked up the book. Its title was *Antiquities of the Church,* edited and published by a William Andrews in 1896.

Of late, the caretaker had not been feeling well, and this experience, shocking as it had been for him, did not improve his condition. Consulting his doctor, Jonas told him the tale, but the physician was skeptical and said it was probably just a hallucination. Jonas then decided he needed another witness with him if he should encounter the ghost—or whoever it was—again. Mr. Willmott, the curator, volunteered to watch with him. So, as the series of religious meetings continued, Willmott stayed with Jonas each Sunday after that for three weeks. However, they saw nothing.

Then on the Sunday evening of October 18, 1953, just a few minutes after Mr. Willmott left the building, George Jonas saw the apparition a second time. The elderly figure came down the stairs from the first floor of the museum, crossed the hall, and passed directly through the closed library door. Jonas opened it and went in. Nowhere was the figure to be seen. He checked the *Antiquities* book, but it had not been disturbed. The time was around 7:40 P.M.

Because the apparition seemed to object to the presence of Mr. Willmott, Jonas asked a friend of his, Walter French, to keep watch with him. On the night of November 15 their vigil was rewarded. As Jonas and French were walking among the book stacks that evening, they both heard the pages of a book being turned. Reaching the center aisle, they discovered the same *Antiquities* book lying on the floor. Its pages were still fluttering. The ghost was not visible on this occasion, but the time—as before—was 7:40 P.M.

At this point, George Jonas was considerably disturbed. He went to his doctor and reported this latest development. The doctor continued to insist that Jonas had seen no ghost; to prove it, he would stand watch with him on the next likely Sunday evening. By this time the spectral manifestations had fallen into a kind of pattern. Something seemed to be either seen or heard on every fourth Sunday. Accordingly, on the night of December 13, Jonas, his doctor, a lawyer, and four other persons stationed themselves in the museum library to await the apparition. One of these seven assembled spectators was James Jonas, George's older brother, a locomotive engineer.

That evening those present could not all watch the *Antiquities* volume, which the ghost seemed most interested in, so they simply circulated about the library. As they had gathered, however, they had first inspected the book closely to make certain it had not been rigged up with wires on its shelf, or been tampered with in any way. On this occasion it turned out to be George Jonas's brother, James, who saw the book in flight. "It didn't seem to fall at the same speed books usually fall," he declared. *Antiquities*, he said, seemed to edge out from its shelf to its full width before it started to descend.

As it landed, James Jonas yelled to the other observers, who immediately dashed to the spot. There, on the floor, the book was seen with its pages turning and fluttering as if in a wind. George Jonas' doctor made a fresh inspection of the shelf with his flashlight. But no threads, strings, or wires were to be seen whereby a hoaxer could have manipulated the volume.

Later, the doctor commented that just prior to the flight of the book he felt a cold, clammy sensation in his legs, but that after the book hit the floor his knees and legs felt fine again. The lawyer present at the vigil commented afterward, "I wouldn't have represented anybody who told me a story like this. But we have the proof of our own eyes."

"Now," George Jonas said to the others assembled that night, "perhaps somebody will believe me."

By this time, the York Museum ghost's activities had reached the newspapers, and reporters began to clamor around the museum gates every Sunday evening, eager for the latest incident. The next Sunday on which the specter was anticipated was January 10; however, on that night Jonas was sick and did not report for duty. Mr. Willmott took up the vigil in the library, but evidently his presence inhibited the apparition's appearing. Nor was the book disturbed at all that evening.

News of the Yorkshire phantom had also reached the British Society for Psychical Research, which asked permission to conduct an investigation of the case on February 7, 1954. Present were several distinguished investigators, including Trevor Hall and Eric Dingwall. On this evening, however, the small Edwardian specter did not appear, and the *Antiquities* volume remained untouched. Also present was James Jonas, who at one point that night thought he saw a disembodied waxen-white hand slithering its way down the bookshelf, as if searching for a book. But he was rather unsure of this, especially when questioned by the noted scientists, and eventually he retreated to the position that it "might have been a trick of the light."

Hall and Dingwall were tough researchers to convince. At length they concluded that although George Jonas had obviously seen some kind of apparition, it may have been a hallucination of his own mind. Furthermore, they said, the book might well have been pulled from the shelf by a rigged-up string or wire. Yet none was ever found. In any event, the apparition was never again seen, either by George Jonas or anyone else.

THE GHOST WHO PLAYED BILLIARDS

ONE OF THE MOST REMARKABLE MULTIPLE-WITNESS APPARI-
tion cases in the annals of English psychic literature happened during World War II in a lovely old home in the
Midlands. It was reported in detail by Lieutenant Colonel
The O'Doneven of Lymington, Hampshire. The unusual
aspect of the case was that the apparition actually participated in a game of billiards with the human being, Colonel
O'Doneven, who was observing it. At the time, however,
the colonel did not realize that his opponent was a ghost.

In the fall of 1943, O'Doneven, an artillery officer, had
taken two field batteries up to the Midlands. The men were
given quarters in various buildings of a nobleman's estate,
while the officers were housed in the main manor house
which was surrounded by many rolling acres of park land.
During daylight drill hours, the batteries used these grounds

to practice-fire their artillery pieces. The officers drove their gun crews hard, for they were soon due to be attached to an infantry division for the coming invasion of Hitler's Fortress Europe.

When Colonel O'Doneven first arrived at the manor house, it was empty except for two old family servants; the owner was away at war and his wife was living elsewhere. All of the furniture and pictures were shrouded in dust-covers. One of the servants, the butler, had been left in charge of the estate for the duration of the war. The butler once confided to O'Doneven that, before the arrival of his troops, the manor house had been briefly occupied by someone else. Upon learning that the house contained a ghost, this man had hurriedly moved elsewhere and had not returned.

The colonel paid little attention to the story, for he was not a man who took stock in ghost tales. Moreover, there was a war on, and he had his men to worry about. Finding himself short of cooks and other personnel, O'Doneven hired the butler to help him form a small officers' mess. In so doing, the colonel hoped also to impress on the butler that he and his men considered themselves guests in the manor house and not intruders. The butler cooperated fully, and in short order the mess was organized, with the main meal in the evening scheduled for 7:45 P.M.

A couple of weeks later at the scheduled time, Colonel O'Doneven was on his way down the stairs that led to the small hall where his officers met for their evening meal. However, in checking a clock on the stairway wall, he saw that it read only 6:45—an hour too early. Thinking that his watch was somehow off by a whole hour, he wondered how he might spend the time until evening mess. It was a chilly autumn night, and he considered sitting before the fire that

burned brightly in the hall where he and his officers took their meals. But, just as he was about to do this, he heard the sounds of clicking billiard balls in an adjoining room. An avid billiards player, the colonel's spirits brightened at the thought of a game.

He pushed open the door and found himself in a room he had not been in before. It was, he noted, a very large room, comfortably accommodating the full-sized billiard table placed in the center. Cue racks lined the walls. Later, he remembered thinking that it resembled the kind of billiard room built for only one table that could still be found in some old taverns.

O'Doneven perceived that there was a player at the table in the act of shooting balls. He appeared to be a youngish man, and he wore Army dress blues which reminded O'Doneven of those worn by General Kitchener's soldiers in World War I. He also noticed that the man was hunchbacked. The young soldier said nothing but continued to knock the balls around the table.

"Want a game?" asked the colonel. The young man still said nothing, but smiled and nodded in assent.

So the game began. Alternating their shots, O'Doneven and the blue-clad soldier continued the game for several minutes. The young man smiled often but he still said nothing. When the score reached 98 to 98, O'Doneven became aware of chairs scraping and the clump of Army boots in the adjoining room. These, he knew, were his officers beginning to assemble for the evening meal in the mess hall.

It was now the colonel's shot—which was an easy one—and he looked forward to racking up the last 2 points to win the game at the score of 100 to 98. Taking deliberate aim with his cue, he cracked off the cue ball and watched it carom off the red ball to the white.

"That's done it," O'Doneven said. "My game."

The colonel watched the young soldier noiselessly put his cue back up in the rack, smile at him, and walk quietly through another door. Later, he learned that the door led into a bathroom.

Rather puzzled, O'Doneven left the billiard room and joined his officers in the mess. As the evening meal progressed, he kept thinking about the odd young man at the billiard table. Half way through dinner, he decided to question his officers.

"I say," he began, "have any of you seen the little chap in the blues?" But none of them had, and O'Doneven was about to let the matter drop when he added, "A nice lad, with a hump. I've just beaten him at billiards."

Just then the colonel noticed that the butler, who was about to serve him some apple tart, seemed to freeze and become very pale. Then he said, "You've seen Master Willie, sir."

By now the colonel sensed that there was something very peculiar going on. He waited and then asked, "Well, man, can't you tell us something more of this Willie?"

The butler swallowed hard and wet his lips. "Master Willie, sir, was her Ladyship's brother. He had managed to join Kitchener's Army in 1915, but the authorities threw him out on discovering that he was deformed. He came back here, Christmas, 1916. He played a good game of billiards and shot himself in the room where he loved to play. We see him sometimes . . ."

Some years after the war, O'Doneven's story came to the attention of a noted researcher and writer on British ghosts. This man arranged an interview with the colonel and questioned him closely on certain points.

"How near did you come to the ghost?" asked the researcher.

"I hardly noticed that," O'Doneven replied, "as it was all so natural. We just went on playing our shots as they came."

The colonel explained that aside from his invitation to play a game, to which the ghost had only replied with a smile, no other words had passed between them—except for O'Doneven's saying that he had won the game.

"Tell me," continued the researcher, "who else saw the man in blue?"

"A few nights later," O'Doneven told him, "two of my subalterns, coming downstairs, spotted the wee figure walking away from the fire. Instead of following, they rushed back upstairs to collect the other subalterns, and possibly more courage, and all tumbled downstairs again to check. There was a light switched on over the billiard table—two lights in fact, but no player. I feel my officers missed a chance."

If only Colonel O'Doneven had seen the apparition, the case would hardly have qualified as a remarkable one. Yet not only had he seen Master Willie, but so also had the butler, members of the family, and the subalterns. Furthermore, the case falls into the category of those in which the apparition, having met an unhappy end, chooses to remain earthbound and haunt the scene of his death for a time before taking up his existence in the afterlife.

THE BROWN LADY OF RAYNHAM HALL

As a so-called "recurring apparition," the ghost known as the Brown Lady of Raynham Hall has been seen from time to time for almost two centuries. Raynham Hall is the Norfolk home of the Marquis of Townshend, and the late Marchioness of Townshend reported that she had seen the apparition several times in this century. The present Marquis, however, claims never to have seen it. But it was seen by the famous English naval officer and novelist Captain Frederick Marryat, and in 1936 a couple of lucky photographers managed to take the apparition's picture.

In what is called the "haunted chamber" at Raynham Hall hangs a painted portrait of the Brown Lady of Raynham. She is wearing a brown satin dress and an elegant ruff. Her eyes are remarkably deep-set, luminous, and faintly evil-looking.

The Brown Lady is distinctly aristocratic, and her hair is done in a neat coif. The peculiar thing about her is that no one in the Townshend family knows who she is—or was.

While the apparition of the woman in the portrait had been seen many times before 1835, it was in that year that the first detailed account of the appearance of the ghost was written by Lucia C. Stone. Mrs. Stone obtained her facts from an eyewitness, and they are generally regarded as accurate.

It was Christmastime at Raynham Hall and a large holiday party was in residence. The guests included Colonel Loftus, his wife, and her cousin, Miss Page. Colonel Loftus was a relative—the brother of the Marchioness and a cousin of the Marquis.

One night just before Christmas, the colonel and another guest, Mr. Hawkins, sat down to play a game of chess. Both men were veteran players, and the match turned out to be a long one. It was well past midnight before the colonel finally managed to defeat Hawkins.

Both men were tired and they went upstairs to bed. They were bidding each other good night when Mr. Hawkins tugged at Colonel Loftus' sleeve and pointed toward the door of the Marchioness's room. The colonel looked in that direction and saw a lady standing there.

"How strangely she is dressed," remarked Mr. Hawkins.

Since Colonel Loftus was nearsighted, he did not immediately see the figure. However, when he had gotten his monocle adjusted, he saw the figure of a woman dressed in clothing of perhaps 100 years before. He watched her walk away down the corridor and slowly fade from sight. Realizing he'd just seen a ghost, he felt his flesh crawl.

Before his visit was over, the colonel saw the strange ghostly figure once again. This time his monocle was in place

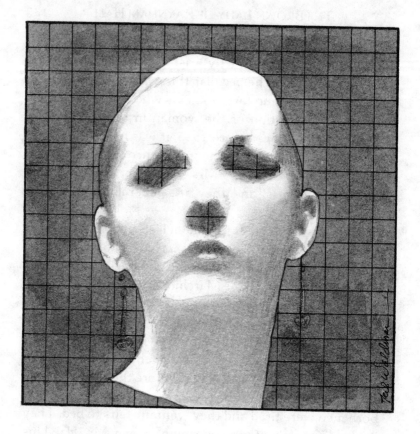

and he got a good look at her. She was again in the upper corridor, proceeding toward the head of the staircase. The colonel was climbing the stairs. Determining this time to outmaneuver her, he quickened his steps so that they soon came face to face. Brave soldier though he was, the colonel was quite shaken at what he saw. Facing him was an aristocratic lady, coiffed and dressed in brown brocade, with her features exuding a kind of ghostly light. The shocking thing about her was her empty, cavernous eye-sockets—for she had no eyes at all!

The next day, the colonel attempted to draw a sketch of

the apparitional Brown Lady. No one laughed at his story, for the Townshend family was accustomed to her infrequent appearances. When Miss Page asked her host whether he believed in the ghost of Raynham Hall, the Marquis replied, "I cannot help but believe, for she ushered me into my room just last night."

A few years later, Captain Marryat, author of many sea stories, had his encounter with the Brown Lady. Raynham Hall had just been redecorated, and he was one of a large party staying at the mansion to celebrate the refurbished old mansion. The captain had heard about the ghost of the Brown Lady, but he refused to take any stock in it.

"Let me sleep in this so-called haunted room," he said scornfully to Lord Townshend. "We'll soon show 'em what nonsense it is."

Accordingly, Marryat was led to the chamber. As he was retiring, he glanced at the portrait of the Brown Lady as it flickered eerily in the candlelight. He had to admit there was something sinister and malevolent-looking about the woman's deep-set eyes. When he had stripped down to his undergarments, he heard a knock on his door, and he let in two young men who were also houseguests. They said there was to be a shooting party the next day, and they wanted some technical advice about their firearms. An avid gunman, Marryat went just as he was—in his underwear—to their rooms in order to inspect the guns. When he had finished, he left for his own chamber, and the two young men accompanied him.

As the trio proceeded along the darkened corridor, all three men suddenly saw the figure of a woman coming toward them. Embarrassed at his state of undress, Marryat hid with his companions behind the door of a vacant room. As he watched the figure get closer, Marryat felt his flesh creep. He recognized it as being the apparition of the Brown

Lady of the portrait hanging in his room. On and on she came, making no noise at all on the solid oak flooring. This time she was holding a lamp whose rays clearly reflected her brown dress. As it glided past the door where he and the young men were partially hidden, the figure turned and gazed at them "in such a diabolical manner," as the captain later wrote, that they were terrified.

At this point, Marryat had little doubt that the figure was a ghost and not human. He happened to be carrying with him a brace of pistols, which he had been showing to the two young men. Pointing one at the phantom, he fired point-blank. His bullet passed directly through the figure, slammed into a door behind her, and embedded itself. With the firing of the bullet, the ghost immediately faded away.

Many years later, in 1926, the reappearance of the apparition created a sensation when the newspapers learned of it. In November of that year, Lady Townshend was in residence at Raynham Hall. She reported that her son and a friend had encountered the Brown Lady on the main staircase. While neither of these young men had been told that the Hall was reputed to be haunted, they both identified the figure they had seen with the portrait hanging in the haunted chamber.

In mid-September of 1936—nearly ten years after young Townshend and his friend met the Brown Lady on the old staircase—the amazing sequel to the Raynham Hall case occurred. Lady Townshend had commissioned two experienced photographers to photograph the entire estate, including the mansion. These men were Captain Provand, the art director, and Indre Shira, of the firm of Indre Shira, Ltd., of London. Shortly after 8 o'clock on September 19, they began to take a large number of pictures of the grounds and house, and by 4 o'clock in the afternoon they were ready to photograph the oak staircase.

Captain Provand took one shot of the staircase while Mr. Shira worked the flashbulb. Then, just as the captain was focusing for another exposure, Shira—flashbulb pistol in hand—stood beside him at the back of the camera, looking right up the staircase. Detecting what he later described as "an ethereal veiled form" moving slowly down the staircase, he shouted out excitedly, "Quick! Quick! There's something! Are you ready?"

The captain answered yes, removed the cap from the lens, and Mr. Shira pressed the flashbulb pistol, which worked at the speed of one-fiftieth of a second. At this point, Provand, mystified at Shira's behavior, asked, "What's all the excitement about?"

Mr. Shira maintained that he had distinctly seen, coming down the staircase, a transparent figure through which the steps could be seen. The captain laughed at this and said he must have been imagining things, for there was now nothing in sight. However, Shira insisted that he had seen a perfectly real, ethereal form of some sort.

On their trip back to London, the two photographers argued and discussed the incident over and over again. Provand claimed that it was impossible to obtain a genuine ghost photograph outside a seance room, and that he would stake his reputation as a court photographer of thirty years' experience on it. Nevertheless, Mr. Shira stoutly affirmed that he had seen a figure on the old oak staircase, and that it must have been caught at the psychological moment by the lens of the camera.

Later they repaired to the darkroom together and developed the negatives one after another. Suddenly Provand exclaimed, "Good Lord, there's something on the staircase negative, after all! Look!" Mr. Shira took one glance and decided to call in a third party as a witness. Mr. Jones, manager of the chemist shop downstairs, arrived just in time to see the negative being taken from the developer and placed in the hypo bath. Mr. Jones, an amateur photographer of some experience, declared that had he not actually seen the negative being fixed he would never have accepted the subsequent picture as genuine. Later the famous English psychic researcher Harry Price examined the negative and cross-examined the photographers. His conclusion was that the photographers had had no reason to fabricate the story, and that the negative was "entirely innocent of any faking."

What was on the famous negative? When printed, it showed a shadowy form of a hooded woman. It was definitely a human figure—not unlike a nun dressed in white, but her face, hands, and feet were not discernible. The folds of her dress could be distinctly seen, and the steps of the oak staircase were clearly visible through the white apparition. Also, her brilliance seemed to be casting highlights on the surrounding woodwork. Subsequently the photograph— one of the best ever obtained of an apparition—was published in the December 26, 1936, edition of *Country Life*.

Psychical researchers consider the Raynham Hall case a significant one because the photographers involved were not in the least interested in occult occurrences, and thoughts of apparitions, ghosts, or phantoms were not in their minds when the event occurred. In recent years, no reappearance of the Brown Lady has been reported. Whoever she was in the dim past, she may have been deeply wronged in some way—perhaps she was even a victim of murder. According to one occult theory, her spirit remained earthbound for some two centuries, feeling somehow compelled to haunt the mansion where the wrong—whatever it was—had taken place.

THE POLTERGEIST OF RUNCORN

THIS CASE, WHICH OCCURRED DURING THREE MONTHS OF 1952 in the north of England, was meticulously documented by the British Society for Psychical Research. Investigators on the spot witnessed furniture doing macabre dances and other weird events. As of that year, such happenings had never been observed by so many independent persons.

The strange occurrences began in August 1952 at 1 Byron Street, a narrow, quiet thoroughfare in the small town of Runcorn. At this address stood a small terraced house, and in it lived a widower, Sam Jones, with his daughter-in-law and his grandson, sixteen-year-old John Glynn. On the day the disturbances began, all three witnesses were in the sitting room when suddenly a small knick-knack rose from a table and flew across the room. Then some books fell from a shelf of their own accord. Mr. Jones, his grandson, and his daughter-in-law watched these events in amazement. But these were only preliminaries of more violent ones to come. On subsequent days, a highboy was seen to rock on its legs and nearly topple over; dishes and silverware took off from their resting places and smashed against walls; pictures dropped from where they were hanging; once a small fire started spontaneously in the kitchen.

Mr. Jones, thinking that somebody must be playing practical jokes on his family, reported the matter to the police. A police sergeant was sent to investigate, and he too witnessed some of the odd occurrences. However, he was powerless to stop them, for no human being seemed to be perpetrating them. A local spiritualist medium was called in and claimed to have made contact with an "entity," but had no success in preventing the poltergeist activity. Day after day the phenomena continued, until the family was in a near state of collapse from nervous anxiety. A Methodist minister in the town who witnessed many of the Byron Street occurrences remarked, "One doubts the evidence of one's senses in these matters."

Eventually word of the strange affair reached the British Society for Psychical Research. Investigators there decided this was a case that ought to be thoroughly looked into—and with as many witnesses present as possible. It was now mid-September, and the Society scheduled a team of investigators to be present at the house at around 11:00 P.M. to observe whatever might take place. That evening proved to be a warm one, and knots of people had already gathered at 1 Byron Street.

The team of Society researchers entered through the open door and made their way upstairs. Since most of the recent disturbances had been centering around sixteen-year-old John Glynn, it had been decided to set up the night's vigil outside the closed door of the big front bedroom where John was sleeping—or at least trying to. John was not alone in the room, however. So alarmed had he become by the nightly occurrences that he had persuaded a friend, John Berry, to share the room with him.

The boys retired about 11:30 P.M., and the observers took up their positions outside in the hallway. It was an odd assembly of people. There were the psychic researchers

holding infra-red cameras with which they hoped to get pictures of any poltergeist events. There were also church ministers, a police sergeant, a radio broadcasting team, and many curious onlookers crowded on the stairway and the floor below. The boys had already switched their light out, all was quiet, and everybody simply waited to see if anything would happen. It soon did.

Promptly at midnight there were sounds of violence in the boys' room. One of the researchers opened the door and powerful flashlight beams were played about the bedroom. Before the terrified eyes of the boys in their beds and the gaze of those crowding into the chamber, objects of furniture were doing a fantastic dance. A dresser was teetering violently and slamming itself against one of the walls; a dressing table was creaking and hopping along the floor; drawers spilling their contents were being heaved across the room; a large cardboard box was jiggling vertically in midair; a book was sailing across the room and was seen to slam into a lamp. By this time several people had entered the bedroom and others crowded the doorway, hall, and stairs. Many, many witnesses were able to see at least part of the incredible activity inside, and the researchers saw it all.

These and more events continued for some minutes, after which there was a lull. A Reverend Stevens recalled what occurred next: "I found a table had moved into the middle of the room. Someone pushed it back against the wall, but it promptly moved out again about six feet. Addressing the table, I said: 'If you can hear my voice, knock three times.' Immediately it began to shake vigorously three times. All in the room saw the rocking table with no one near it. The two boys were lying in bed on the far side of the room. I went to see if the table would rock of its own accord, but it was firm on the floor."

It was not long after this that the activity began anew—and with increased ferocity. A number of articles left the dressing table and clattered on the floor; a drawer was flung across the room and dumped its contents at the foot of a bed; a tablecloth was ripped from end to end; an alarm clock smashed into pieces on the floor. The night's poltergeist activity eventually ended with a chilling finale: young John Glynn's pillows were suddenly plucked out from under him, and the boy was then thrown out of bed and onto the floor. He later claimed that he was in the grip of some powerful force which he could not resist. All present agreed he looked petrified by the violent experience. During this and other incidents, declared the police sergeant, John seemed to be in a state of near nervous collapse. And, added the sergeant, " ... those boys aren't doing it, believe me. I'm not strong enough to make that table dance about as it has done, and I'm sure the boys could not do it."

The uncanny poltergeist disturbances went on night after night. Some were unusually violent in nature. On one occasion when the lights in the room were out, ornaments, books, and other items were flung about with such force that they dented and nicked the walls. When an investigator switched on the lights, observers witnessed a box containing a jigsaw puzzle rising up through the air toward the ceiling. At the time, the two boys were lying in bed with blankets over them. A few seconds later, the box smashed with a loud crack on the floor. Fortunately, Society researchers were able to photograph this event.

Needless to say, the investigators remained suspicious of the two boys, since the disturbances were obviously centering about them. The chief mission of their investigation was to determine whether they were guilty of hoax or fraud. So the room was thoroughly searched each night. For their part, the boys cooperated fully and submitted to any test the scientists asked—even to tying up their hands and feet. Once two Society men held John Glynn so that he could not touch anything. While they were doing so, the dressing table was seen to rock violently, as was a heavy cedar chest. But never were the two boys caught in any trickery or prank-playing.

By Christmas, the strange events began to peter out and then they stopped altogether. No longer did crowds gather outside 1 Byron Street, and scientists and reporters ended their vigil. The men from the Society all agreed that no human activity seemed to be responsible for the mysterious happenings. If there had been fraud in the house on Byron Street, it would have had to be remarkably sophisticated. The scientists' report to the Society for Psychical Research reflected their puzzlement over these inexplicable happenings: "That these disturbances were not caused by human agency, we are firmly convinced. During one particularly noisy period, we saw and obtained photographs of the dressing table several inches in the air.

"There is no logical explanation for such occurrences. For want of any better explanation, we must attribute the disturbances to poltergeist phenonema."